The Adventures of Francie Fitzgerald

A Novel by

Victoria Kamar Olivett

Joshua Tree
Publishing

• Chicago •

The Adventures of Francie Fitzgerald
Victoria Kamar Olivett

Published by
Joshua Tree Publishing
• Chicago •
JoshuaTreePublishing.com

13-Digit ISBN: 978-1-941049-08-2

Cover Photo: Woman ©natali_mya
Dog ©byrdyak

Disclaimer:
This is a work of fiction. Names, characters, places, and incidents are the product of the author's imagination or have been used fictitiously. Any resemblance to actual persons, living or dead, events, locales or organizations is entirely coincidental.

Printed in the United States of America

Dedication

"Scientific discovery knows no country. It's knowledge is for humanity, and it is the torch which illuminates the world."
—Louis Pasteur

This book is dedicated to my husband Daniel, my daughters Rosemary, Teresa, and Monica and my grandchildren Lily, Joe, Anna, Maria, Danica, Danny, Victoria, and Veronica and others yet to come. Thank you to all of the children I have taught over the years and all of my wonderful grandkids for inspiring me to never lose my imagination. If you can imagine it, you can achieve it.

A book is the doorway to exploration.

Chapter 1

1885

Collin is crying so loudly this morning. It would be really nice to sleep in just once in a while around this place! As I walk into the kitchen, I grab a cup of black coffee and sit down at the table. As usual, Mother adds lots of milk into my steaming cup.

"Good morning, Francie. How are you this beautiful morning?"

"I feel good. Just a little tired, Mother. How did you sleep?"

"Collin woke up a couple of times during the night, but he went right back to sleep," Mother responds.

"Mama, I am almost done reading the book *Treasure Island*. I am trying to read as many books as I can this summer to prepare for going to Newark High School in the fall. I can't wait to go there!"

Before Mother can respond, Aunt Molly has to saunter into the kitchen and put her two cents into my life as usual. She has a scowl on her face and rarely smiles. Her shoulders are hunched over, and she waddles each time she takes a step.

"Francie, you don't need to worry about all the fancy education you want. You are just a girl of fourteen, and as a good Irish girl, you need to concentrate on learning how to take care of the home, cook, and clean. Save the education for your brother Austin."

"Well, Aunt Molly, I don't agree with anything you are saying. I am as smart as any boy. I have such a desire to learn, and nobody is going to stop me! I will be the first girl in our family to graduate from high school."

I quickly finish my coffee. I just have to get outside and get away from this tenement in Newark and away from Aunt Molly as soon as possible!

"Mother, I am going for a walk since it is so beautiful outdoors," I remark quickly as I give my little brother Collin a kiss on his forehead as he is now finally sitting calmly down in his high chair, smiling while holding his little blue teddy bear.

I step out of the old brown brick building with a quick jump off the porch; I can't believe how Aunt Molly is trying to ruin yet another day in my life. Oh well, soon she will be gone to Morristown to work at the O'Briens' house all day, and she will be gone by the time I get back from my walk.

Sometimes I feel like I will suffocate if I don't get out of our apartment. I take a deep breath and begin moving quickly toward the lake. The wind is pointing the cedar trees toward the path to the cemetery on the hill, so maybe I should take a minute and go there; the calm landscape may help my mood.

I stop and pay my respects to Grandma and Grandpa Sullivan, who came to this country many years ago from Ireland. Colleen and Michael are lying next to each other for eternity in front of an old Irish cross that stands behind them. It has a round circle, which represents the sun of the old Irish beliefs, placed inside of a cross. Tears come to my eyes as I softly say a prayer. I very much miss my grandmother.

As I look around, I see lots of Irish names engraved on headstones. Many, I'm sure, were killed in the Civil War. There are Egans, Gleasons, and Murphys, just to name a few. The headstones seem to go on and on through the deep green grass, spreading like a roll call of those who have passed away. I also see tombstones smoothed with age; sadly, their names are no longer visible and will never be remembered.

Taking a deep breath, I start moving slowly toward the lake. As I get closer, the breeze from the water hits my face, blowing my hair every which way. The dew is blanketing the wild pink and hazel crocuses blooming under an apple tree. Their lovely, sweet fragrance is welcoming, and a small yellow goldfinch takes flight to a nearby evergreen. The water is sparkling majestically in the sun's reflection. The tranquil blue sky is mirroring itself in the splendid sea. It is so calming here.

The bass are jumping high above the water, catching insects for their morning breakfast. A spotted, darling fawn near the woods runs off when he hears me approach. I browse at the buzzing bees bouncing boldly from one bright sunflower to the next. A tiny blue hummingbird drinks nectar from a red xenia. There is such a magic to it all, a connection and splendor, that I just have to be part of it all this morning.

I relax so much when I'm here. I know there is more to life than the chores I do daily. Learning gives me such joy, and if I can help others with knowledge, then so be it. I will decide my own future. I am so determined. I am not going to let anyone or anything discourage me from fulfilling my dreams, especially Aunt Molly.

As I turned around to leave this calm, tranquil stretch of land by the lake, I am startled by the ugly sight of a dead fox lying right next to me in the brush near the path through the woods. The odor is appalling, flies are everywhere, and his dead eyes are staring directly at me as foam drips from his open mouth. Of course, I let out an awful scream and run home as fast as I can, feeling a little sick from the awful odor I have just inhaled.

As I get to the steps of our apartment, out of breath, I open the door and hear Mother's gentle voice as she is rocking little Collin in her arms and singing:

"When Irish eyes are smiling, sure 'tis like a morn in spring.
In the lit of Irish laughter, you can hear the angels sing.
When Irish hearts are happy, all the world seems bright and gay.
And when Irish Eyes are smiling, sure they steal your heart away."

I feel better now that I am finally home. I watch Mother as she puts him back in the high chair and gives him oatmeal and fruit.

"He loves the berries you picked yesterday, Francie. Would you like some breakfast, my dear?"

"No thanks, not right now," I say as my stomach is still queasy.

I have to walk over and give the boy a big hug and give him a kiss on his chubby cheek. He's a year and a half old and so enjoying the blueberries, which are now smudged all over his blue mouth. I feel ashamed now that yesterday I complained so much because I had to take care of him all afternoon.

Sitting by him at the kitchen table, I look up at my beautiful mother, Meg (Margaret Colleen), with her long red hair put neatly in a bun on the top of her head. I see her gleaming green eyes, but today she looks somehow different. Mama wears her hair like that all the time too. Also, I see her often in that faded brown blouse and long skirt covered with that same old stained yellow apron. I guess I don't always appreciate my mother. She is continually there for me and makes me feel better about everything, and just being here with her, I feel so much better.

The cheerful sunshine is now bringing its morning warmth into our kitchen, brightening the light golden room. A summer breeze is blowing through the opened window, moving the green curtains lazily back and forth. The coffee pot sits on the old stove, brewing much of the time, as coffee is the main refreshment in the Fitzgerald household. Mother hands me my second cup of coffee for the day. I laugh as the cup is almost completely white with all the cream she keeps adding. The icebox in the corner of the room is continually growling as if it is forever hungry.

Our kitchen is where our family communicates and expresses our feelings about the world in which we live. Around that big old wooden kitchen table in the center of the room is where we partake both our meals and family conversations about the goings-on of the day. Mother always encourages all of us to share our ideas and opinions about what is happening in the world and discuss things we do at school when we sit down for dinner.

The yellow and white daisies protruding from the flowered green vase sitting in the center of the table are now sparkling in the day's sunlight. As Mother begins singing another verse of "When Irish Eyes Are Smiling," all seems right with the world.

My younger brother Austin darts into the room, quickly bouncing into a chair while grabbing a piece of darkened toast at the same time. He can't wait to go outside and play with his chums, and being ten, he is the oldest of the group. Austin looks so much like Mother. He and Collin have her auburn hair, while Mary, my younger sister, and I have black hair like our dad, Paddy.

Daddy (Patrick Ryan Fitzgerald) is working at the shoe factory in the "Down Neck" section of Newark near the iron factories. This is an area of the city where many of the immigrants work since there are a lot of workshops in that part of town. The industries have brought lots of newcomers to Newark. Daddy especially likes working the double shifts at the factory to make extra money for our family. Our father is tall and, with his bright blue eyes, quite handsome. Daddy was born on March 17, the feast day of Saint Patrick; it's quite fitting that he has the saint's name.

Austin quickly drinks his milk, leaving a white mustache over his lips. "Mother, can I go outside to play?"

"Finish your chores first, my boy. You have to take the rubbish out to the backyard barrel and clean up the mess you and your friends made out there yesterday."

"Okay, Mama. I will do it after breakfast," replies Austin.

"Mother, where is Mary this morning?" I ask.

"She's next door, babysitting at the O'Connors'," Mother replies as Collin runs outside to do his work.

"Mother, on my walk by the lake, I saw a dreadful sight this morning," I explained.

"What was it, Francie?"

"I saw a dead fox in the brush. I have seen dead animals before, but this is nothing like I have ever seen. Its wide, bulging eyes stared right at me, and there was foam coming out of its opened mouth. It had many bites all over its body, and its fur was soaked in its own blood," I explain further.

"I wonder what happened to that poor animal!" reflects Mother.

"Mama, I wonder that, too. I am going to go to the parlor for a while."

The small front room of our apartment is really not a formal sitting area, but the family likes to call it the parlor since it is such an important part of our home. It has a pocket door that slides out of the wall when you want to close off the room. There is crown molding at the ceiling and a big window overlooking Union Street. The room is so comfortable, and this is where I go to do my most profound thinking and where I write down my most personal thoughts in my diary.

Through the large glass window in the front, I can see the residents of Newark hurriedly promenading down our street. As I gaze outside, I see the excitement of our city moving right in front of our place. Someday, I would like to be part of all this enthusiasm. They are all hurrying about their business. Men are walking with their round straw hats, dark suits, and wide ties. Women, with their ruffles, bows, and long dresses, stroll by briskly in the morning's light.

I notice that there are also several dogs in a pack, running swiftly down the street, barking loudly. We seem to have a lot of stray dogs around here at all hours of the day, and each day, more seem to show up in our neighborhood.

As I slump down on the old leather chair Daddy got at the secondhand store, I see the tattered couch that belonged to Grandma leaning against the faded silver wallpaper on the far wall. Looking at the sofa, I am reminded of Grandma Colleen again today. There in the corner is a heap of old newspapers piled high on the old bookcase next to the window. Daddy gets the papers from a friend at work. He loves to read them in his spare time since they have so many interesting articles.

Leaning back on the chair and closing my eyes for a second, I still cannot get that disgusting image of the fox out of my mind. The next time I see Sean, I must tell him about this morning, and maybe he can figure out what happened to that poor animal. I take out my diary from the little table by the couch and begin describing my adventure.

Now I can hear Mother calling me, of course. I can't even get five minutes to sit down and do what I want. I envy all those individuals I've seen this morning going somewhere with a purpose. Oh well! Duty calls again.

"The baby is getting fussy, honey. Can you hold him for a minute while I put on the supper?" asks Mother.

"If you're making your famous potato leek soup, I will be glad to mind the baby."

The broth is yellow and creamy and looks as good as it smells. Since it is made with potatoes, it is part of a traditional Irish diet. I am memorizing Mother's recipe, seeing now how to make this meal myself one day and carry on our family custom. The wonderful aroma goes through the whole apartment. It's funny how certain smells remind us immediately of something or someone from the past. Now it is as if my grandmother Colleen is here, making dinner for our family. I have the most wonderful memories of her since she was the sweetest grandmother. I remember that she made the most delightful chocolate cookies; her laugh was so loud and contagious, too. She was short and heavy in stature, and when she laughed, I could feel her body shake while she held me tightly in her arms. I will always remember her kind smile and her kindness.

"Mother, when you started boiling the potatoes and cutting up those huge onions, I can see Grandma standing in front of the stove, making her delectable soup. I miss her so very much."

"We have a saying in our family," Mother explains. "Our loved ones who have passed on are never very far from us. Their memories and spirit are eternally with us even now. There isn't a day I don't think of my parents, honey." Mother seems to be looking far away to a distant time as she begins to reminisce while slicing bits of garlic and throwing them into the boiling pot. "Your grandma and grandpa came over from Killarney when they were very young," Mother explains.

"Was it difficult for them to come to America, Mama?" I ask because I have never heard their story before.

"They left because life had been so hard for them. They were willing to make the terrible journey across the ocean," Mother continues. "They were always so poor, and then the potato famine hurt the crops in Ireland. The farmers there relied on growing potatoes because they grew well in Ireland's rocky soil and cool climate. When the potato blight came, though, it ruined all their fields. After that, there was very little for those poor souls to eat except for cabbage or some seaweed from the sea. Thousands died from the great starvation. Then there were lots of sicknesses, also. Many died not only from hunger but also from typhoid, with the high fevers and red spots all over their bodies. Some also got smallpox, which is very similar and just as contagious. They suffered such intestinal miseries, and most didn't survive."

"What did your folks do when they finally got here to America?" I ask because Mother is in such a talkative mood.

"Most Irish would take any job if they could, but many were not treated very well. Some factories had signs saying 'Irish

Need Not Apply.' Life was not easy in the new country, but like all immigrants, they came here for a better life for their children. Lots of the Irish worked in the building trades. Some even built the Brooklyn Bridge, which took many years to finish. Some even died while working on it. Lots passed on from diseases when they got here also because there wasn't hygienic sanitation or clean drinking water in the cities," she adds. "Our life was so much better here in America even though it wasn't very easy because there were more opportunities for families. We didn't have to rely on crops anymore to make a living. Here we have more control over our future."

"Not long after they got here in Newark, my papa, Michael, enlisted in Company K of the Seventh Volunteers of New Jersey and fought for the North in the Civil War," Mother explains. "Papa was proud, so proud to serve our country. Sadly, a minié ball shot from a rebel musket took off part of his leg at the Battle of Gettysburg. They said it wasn't the shot that killed him but the poison of a dirty wound. His leg had developed gangrene. That's when the tissues in the body die from the infection. He didn't live much longer after he was wounded."

"I feel so bad that he had to suffer, Mama. I wish I could have gotten to know Grandpa. He was really a hero and a good man to enlist for a cause he believed in," I remark. I can see Mama's green eyes tearing up, thinking about her father.

"I was so young when he passed on," she continues. "He was one of the many casualties of the Battle of Gettysburg. They said there were thousands that died there in Pennsylvania. I will always remember our beloved President Abraham Lincoln and what he said in his Gettysburg Address about those many who sacrificed their lives for our country. Your Grandpa Sullivan was one of those who gave up his life for a 'new birth of freedom.' We will always remember those young men and all they gave up for America."

"I wish there was something that could be done then to help Grandpa," I remark. "So many have died that way from infections. It's very sad. Lots of people do not make it home out of surgery today because of that very reason. Some are afraid to go to the hospital for fear they will not make it back home. In the future, I would like to learn all I can, and maybe I can help others who are suffering as well."

"That's a great goal to have, my girl. I am so proud of you, and I know someday you will accomplish everything you've ever dreamed ."

Mama walks over to the stove with her big spoon, and after tasting the soup, she adds more salt and some fresh parsley. While she stirs the broth, which is simmering slowly, it gives off such a pleasing aroma that I feel like I could eat my supper right this minute.

While I am rocking little Collin, I kiss him softly as he falls asleep in my arms. Putting him in his crib, I swaddle him with his favorite checkered-blue-and-white blanket and lay him gently down for a nap. The satin border has become ragged on the edges of the cover from both the Fitzgerald boys' use, but Collin doesn't seem to mind as he is now sleeping.

Chapter 2

While little Collin is sleeping soundly in his crib, I am thinking this is the time I can get away again to the parlor. As I'm glancing out the large front window, which is now bringing in the bright sunlight, I see the full green branches of the old oak in our front yard, swaying in the summer's gentle wind.

Suddenly, I see Sean now climbing up the stairs to our apartment. I am so glad to see him! He is, without a doubt, my very best friend in the whole wide world.

"Mother!" I yell as I run into the kitchen, "Sean is on the steps outside on the front porch!"

"Shh, Francis, the baby is taking his nap!" Mother reminds me as she walks over to the front door.

"Oh, sorry, Mama. I forgot!"

"Come in, Sean," Mother says as she opens the screen door to let him in.

"How are you doing, Sean?" she asks, looking up at him as he walks through the doorway, bowing his head a little as he steps into the kitchen. "I'm doing great, Mrs. Fitzgerald. How are you this fine day?"

"I'm enjoying these warm summer days. I wish we could always have such fine weather in Newark."

I dart into the other room, so excited that he has stopped over today. "Sean, I am so glad you are here! Did you get off work early?"

"Mr. O'Malley said I can take a couple of hours off before I have to come back later to help close the store. Is everything okay, Francie?"

"Well, I saw something very unusual as I was walking this morning to the lake. It kind of frightened me," I explained.

"What was it, Francie?"

As we walk into the parlor, I begin telling him about the horrible sight I came upon this morning near the lake. Sean is always so smart about sorting things out; I know he will help me figure out what happened. He is in his second year at the high school where I will be attending in the fall. Sean wants to go to Seton Hall College in South Orange, New Jersey, when he gets out of school. He is working very hard so one day he will become a doctor. He is such a good student and has a very positive effect on me with my studies as well. As Sean sees the stack of papers near the window, he suggests we look through the mound of newspapers on the bookcase to look for evidence that may explain what happened to the animal.

As we walked over to the pile of newspapers, we see a variety of *New York Times* editions yellowing with age and all mixed together on the old wooden bookcase. We each take a section of the paper, flop down on the old worn-out couch, and begin researching to find any clue to solve the mystery. After a short time, this seems to be a rather tedious exercise, and my neck is beginning to ache.

After several minutes of browsing, Sean sees a title that grabs his attention as he continues reading the whole column.

"Look, Francie!" says Sean with a serious frown in the middle of his forehead. I look down at his copy of the *New York Times* dated June 1881. The title says, "BOY DIES OF HYDROPHOBIA." These frightening words seem to shout at me as we begin analyzing the article together.

An eleven-year-old boy in New York City was bitten by a dog weeks earlier that must have been infected with rabies. Rabies is a disease of the brain and nervous system, which is caused by the bite of an infected animal who has contracted the illness.

The boy, Frederick Herrman Kruger, was trying to fight off a mad dog when the animal bit him in the face. The bite required several stitches to reattach his nose. The incident was forgotten until later when Frederick became very thirsty playing outdoors but was unable to drink cold tap water. The boy's mother tried to give him some more water that was much warmer, but Frederick still could not drink any of the liquid.

Hence, the term *rabies* is also called hydrophobia, which means "fear of water." The illness does something to the facial muscles so the victims are unable to drink. Also, the boy began having convulsions, which is when muscles shake or spasm. The sickness also causes people to hallucinate or imagine things. While Herrman was suffering, he thought there were dogs hiding under his bed, waiting to attack. This is probably another reason why the boy kept screaming as he lay dying.

The doctors gave Frederick lots of medicine for the pain, but they could not save him. Kruger lived at 380 West Forty-Second Street. Frederick died at the age of eleven.

"Oh, that poor boy and his family," I replied sadly. "That is so tragic. Sean, I am even more terrified than I was earlier today!"

"Francie, I don't know how to tell you this," he says as he grabs my hand, "but I think your fox had a real bad case of rabies. He must have been bitten by some diseased animal. Do you see all the dogs running wild in the neighborhood? The cities of Newark and New York City, for that matter, are still having a lot of trouble controlling the hundreds of stray dogs that are constantly running freely all over our cities."

"Sean, I am really worried about Austin. He is always outdoors, especially in the summer. I feel such anxiety now with the very thought of rabies close by."

"Francie, you are looking awfully pale."

"Sean, I am so nervous that now I am shaking. What are we to do? There are so many children running around the area since it is summer vacation, and I see so many dogs around at any time of night or day."

Sean hugs me and holds me ever so tightly with his strong arms, and I can't help but cry, thinking about poor Herrman.

"It's scary," agrees Sean. "But, Francie, we have to try to live normally in our day-to-day lives and be aware of our surroundings and what is going on around us, my girl. We need to be strong. Try not to think about what happened to the boy in New York. Try only to think of pleasant thoughts that make you smile, Francie."

Sean goes into the kitchen and brings me a cold drink of water. I try to calm down, but I am still having difficulty breathing.

After a while, I respond, "Yes, you are right, Sean, but I can't get that disgusting image from this morning out of my mind. I still see the shaggy fox soaking in blood near the woods, staring at me with those terrifying eyes and the foam still dripping from its mouth. So I guess I just have to try to live with it and keep those dreadful images out of my mind."

"Speaking of thinking of pleasant thoughts, Francie, I almost forgot to tell you! I came over to let you know that Mr. O'Malley is giving me some time off Friday so we can go together to meet the French steamer *Isere* in New York Harbor. The ship is bringing the Statue of Liberty all the way from France to the United States. That is the most thrilling thing we have heard in a long time!" exclaims Sean with a wide grin. Now we are getting up from the couch, hand in hand, just looking into each other's eyes.

Suddenly, as I take another deep breath and another drink of water, my frame of mind is slowly starting to improve. The exciting news is comforting, and with the talk of going to New York City, I am now smiling from ear to ear. Sean, too, is thrilled. He grabs my hands and joins me in a dance as I am now jumping up and down. We cannot stop laughing!

What a joyful moment to put me in better spirits. It is just what I need at this point in time to help me forget about this morning. We have been waiting a long time for this lovely lady to come to our shores, and I can't wait to see her since we helped donate money for her pedestal so she has a place to stand in New York Harbor.

"Mr. O'Malley is expecting me back at the store soon," Sean explains.

Sean has a cup of coffee at the kitchen table before he has to leave for work. I'm certainly now in a much better mood than when he arrived. I try to put today's adventure in the back of my mind and think only about tomorrow. Before we know it, Mary arrives home from babysitting next door.

Then Austin comes running through the front, shouting, "I'm so hungry! Something smells really good!" The door slams behind him.

After the kids finish their chores, it's finally time to enjoy dinner. As we are sitting around the table, I barely say anything while I enjoy the delicious hot soup. Daddy is working the second shift and will eat his supper later. Taking a bite of some scrumptious soda bread that is still warm from the oven, I again think of my grandmother.

"Mama, this bread tastes just like Grandma's," I observed. "It tastes heavenly with the broth."

"I always use my mother's recipes," Mama agrees. "Grandma was the best cook ever!"

As I slowly savor the soup, I look up at Austin. He is such a defenseless little boy who plays outside all the time, and I am so worried as he may have been out there today near some sick animal that could have really hurt him or one of his friends!

"Austin, when you are outdoors, do you see a lot of stray dogs running about?" I ask.

"Yes, there were a lot of them on the corner near Eddie's house today. There must have been at least twenty on his street, and they took off racing right near where we were playing," Austin explains.

"Don't get too close to those dogs or any wild animals in the area as some of them might be sick and mean," I plead.

I don't want him to be fearful to play out in the neighborhood, but he needs to be aware of what is going for his own safety, just as Sean explained. I cringe at the thought of the many dogs always around. I eat my soup slowly, hoping it will give me comfort.

"Okay, Francie, I will try to watch out for those strays, but they seem to be everywhere," he says after dunking some soda bread in his soup.

After dinner, Mary and I clean off the table and wash the dishes while Mother bathes little Collin, getting him ready for bed. After the kitchen is cleaned and the dinner dishes are dried and put away, Mary and I head to the parlor. I need to explain to her about the fox and poor Herrman and the wild dogs. I am having difficulty telling her, as I can see by the look on her face, that she is becoming frightened, especially about the part when the fox is lying in its own blood. It is awful to tell a sixth-grader such news. Her expression becomes sad, and I hate to explain this tonight before she goes to sleep.

"I'm glad you told me, Francie, and I will try to be more careful when I'm outdoors," replies Mary.

"Well, I won't be here in the morning, so I had to warn you tonight, little sister. I am sorry I had to tell you just before you're going to bed."

"That's okay, Francie. I am going to try reading my book, and that will help me to go to sleep."

After an hour, I see Mary closing her book.

"Well, I finished it, Francie, so I am going to turn in now. Good night. I hope you have fun tomorrow in the city," she remarks as she forces a smile.

"Good night, Mary. I am going to bed, too. Yes, I am so looking forward to it."

Even though I am so tired, I can't seem to fall asleep, tossing and turning. I am so excited just thinking about our journey to New York City tomorrow. Finally, I must have fallen asleep, and what seems a very short time later, I am awakened by the bright orange sun rising in the eastern sky. I try not to think about the dead animal from yesterday, but it's the first thing I thought of when I awoke this morning and the last thing I thought of when I went to sleep last night.

Once I am up, I put on my new frilly white blouse and my long blue skirt that I always wear on special occasions. To top it off, I have borrowed Mama's red, white, and blue scarf. Won't I look patriotic! When I walk into the kitchen, I see Daddy sitting at the table, sipping his coffee. I am so glad to see him! I can't wait to have a moment alone with him, finally. He seems either to be always working or together with the whole family.

"Well, my girl, you are up mighty early this morning," Daddy exclaims.

"Sean and I are going to take the ferry to New York, Daddy," I explained.

Then when I want to talk to Daddy alone, of course, Aunt Molly walks into the kitchen. Her shoulders are drooping, which makes her appear shorter than she actually is. Wearing all black, as she always does out of respect for Uncle Frank's passing a couple of years ago, her mood is always somber. Uncle Frank died in an accident in the factory, something my aunt will probably never get over.

As she pours herself a hot cup of coffee, and while adding fresh cream and lots of sugar, she says, "Good morning to you both."

"Good morning, Molly. You are going early to Morristown?" asks Daddy.

"They are having a big party tonight at Mrs. O'Brien's house, so I need to help set up. I will have to leave soon. What are you doing up so early, Francie?" she asks in her usual meddlesome tone.

"Sean and I are going to the harbor to see the French steamer come into port in New York with the Statue of Liberty all the way from France," I answer.

"Francie, why would you want to go down there? There will be a huge crowd of people pushing and shoving. There will be pickpockets, and heaven knows who else might be on the docks," she explains.

Of course, Aunt Molly's remarks bring a negative feeling to my very soul. My shoulders droop as much as hers do. My smile is disappearing. I am standing here in disbelief that a daughter of immigrants could be so critical of the very idea of what we are planning to do today!

After slowly sipping his steaming black coffee, Daddy finally says something. He always thinks before he speaks, and softly he explains his feelings. "Well, Molly, since I am very thankful that I live in this country and I have such opportunities our people didn't have in Ireland, I think Francie has a fine idea. They are going to place that statue on the dock, put her together, and set her in the harbor for all of us to see. Now, won't that be grand, Molly?" Daddy asks.

"Oh, I guess so," she quips with a big frown on her forehead as she gulps down the rest of her coffee, grabs her huge black purse off the kitchen chair, and says "So long!" as she goes out the door.

"Daddy, Aunt Molly has to comment about everything I do. It is so hard to live with a third parent. She tends to spoil my day whenever she gets a chance!" I can feel my face turning bright red, and I am very upset.

"My darling, Aunt Molly is quite lonely and misses Uncle Frank a great deal. Your aunt puts in a long day in Morristown and is not around the house that much. You need to just be more patient with her, Francie."

As I reach for the large block of Swiss cheese from the icebox, I begin to cut two pieces for our lunches I am making for our excursion. Also, I see some melon that will be a nice treat. Next, I slice bread from a loaf of rye that's in the bread box. I begin making sandwiches, and I can't help but think that my parents don't understand how much Aunt Molly interferes in my life. She is nagging me and continually putting my ideas and dreams down. I decide not to discuss my feelings any further this morning, so I just continue getting everything ready to take to the city.

"Daddy, I will be leaving soon so we can get to the ferry before it gets too crowded. I want to go to the harbor in time to see them unload the Statue of Liberty."

I see Sean out front, so I have to leave.

"Have fun today, my girl, and tell me later all about your day," he requests. "I wish I could go with you!"

I give Daddy a big hug, grab the paper sack filled with our lunches, and race out the door to meet Sean. He looks so handsome this morning in his tan waistcoat and dark-brown trousers and his round straw hat. His sparkling brown eyes match his outfit perfectly. I suddenly don't remember anything that Aunt Molly said.

Chapter 3

As Sean and I stroll down Union Street to hop on the trolley, I begin to remember all the ways Americans donated money to help pay for the pedestal for our Statue of Liberty the French people are giving to our country today. Many of our citizens had to scrape up their pennies, dimes, and nickels so there would be something for our beautiful Lady to rest on in New York Harbor.

"Remember, Francie, when you worked all day for Mrs. Ryan for three dollars so you could contribute?"

"I recall, Sean, that day when you worked extra hours for Mr. O'Malley to help the cause too."

"You know, Francie, you and I were like every other person in the country, working so hard so new immigrant families could be welcomed by the beautiful Statue of Liberty."

"Sean, don't you think that was a great idea by Joseph Pulitzer to print every name of every donor in the newspaper *New York World*?"

"It certainly was, Francie. Listing the names of all those individuals who contributed to the fund really encouraged others to give, and people were so excited to see all those generous donors in print in his newspaper," he adds.

"Sean, can you believe that they were able to collect over $100,000 even though most donations were less than a dollar?"

"That kindergarten class in Iowa managed to scrape up a dollar for the pedestal," explains Sean.

"I thought that was the sweetest thing!" I replied, smiling.

"Wealthy citizens didn't really join in the fundraising. If we waited for them to give money, they would not be putting the Statue of Liberty together today," Sean replies.

As we get closer to the trolley, we see lots of people walking toward our ride to the boat. We have to get there soon so we don't miss the ship's arrival at the dock.

"Come on, Francie! Let's make a run for it to the trolley," Sean hollers. Sean is grabbing my hand, making me run as fast as I can to catch up with his long strides.

We make it! As we walk up the steps, we see that there is standing room only. We grab the front handles that are next to the first seats. I am so giddy right now that I begin to laugh. Sean starts laughing, too. Before long, we march off the trolley on Ferry Street, and there is the ferryboat straight ahead, waiting to take us to the harbor. I'm so glad we didn't miss our ride. Looking out to the sea, I am amazed by all the sparkling white sand on the shore near the glistening blue water.

We are some of the first to get off, and we see the ferry right in front of us. Sean holds my arm as we make a mad dash to get on the craft. The strong smell of fish permeates the air, making me a little nauseated. As we climb up the steps, the boat keeps swaying back and forth, which certainly doesn't help my queasiness. I feel as though we are on a sailing ship bound for a faraway land. We have been on such an adventure this morning. The water is such a majestic aqua, and the wind is cooling, so my stomach feels a little better.

As we travel closer and closer to the dock, the grand vessel becomes larger and larger. Butterflies flutter in my stomach. I am so excited. I have never been so close to such a magnificent ship. I cannot believe that we are amidst throngs of people who are waving little American flags, welcoming the French vessel. In front of us, in the clear blue-green sea, is the mighty *Isere*. The smokestacks are billowing big black smoke high into the sky, and suddenly, we hear the booming sound of the ship's horn.

It is as if the French people are here in person, extending their beautiful gift, the Statue of Liberty, to America, which the French call *Liberty Enlightening the World*. Soon, the men are unloading the precious cargo; boxes and boxes are now being lifted out of the ship and placed on the wharf right in front of us. They are opening large crates, and then they take out the Lady's huge arm and torch, her head, and her body.

As they begin to put her together right on the dock, I suddenly remember the beautiful poem "The New Colossus," which Emma Lazarus wrote for a pedestal fundraiser recently in New York City:

> *Here at our sea-washed sunset gates shall stand*
> *A mighty woman with a torch, whose flame*
> *Is the imprisoned lightning, and her name*
> *Mother of Exiles. From her beacon-hand*
> *Glows world-wide welcome; her mild eyes command . . .*
> *Give me your tired, your poor,*
> *Your huddled masses yearning to breathe free,*
> *The wretched refuse of your teeming shore.*
> *Send these, the homeless, the tempest-tost to me,*
> *I lift my lamp beside the golden door!*

These words are so fitting and profoundly speak what all of us here today are thinking. I hope that someday I learn to express myself and the many feelings and emotions I have as wonderful as she does in this verse. This is why I want to be educated, because it is so important to understand everything that is happening in our world. I also want to be able to express ideas eloquently as she does. Emma Lazarus is an example of how women can be determined to help change our world for the better. The Statue of Liberty is a strong and beautiful woman that symbolizes the greatness that lies in every woman.

There are so many individuals on the dock, cheering and laughing. What a joyous occasion! I can't believe how many people are here. Old folks are softly walking on the green grass, and little children are waving flags of red, white, and blue as they run all over the park. This is an experience I will never forget.

Sean holds my hand tightly in his; it is such an emotional and tender moment. Now looking into my eyes, seeing my tears, he places a soft kiss upon my cheek. Suddenly, I put my arms around him, holding him ever so close, and we say nothing. This moment, too, I shall always remember. Although we are surrounded by hundreds, it is as if we are here all alone, just the two of us.

"Francie, I am so glad we were able to be here together today. I am also so proud, too, that we had a chance to contribute to this wonderful event and that we can be a part of it all."

"Yes, Sean, even though ours was a small gift, all the small gifts added up to such a contribution! We can accomplish anything in life if we work together."

The sun is now directly overhead, beaming down its warmth on the entire crowd. The weather is also contributing to this exquisite day. The clear blue skies, the matching sea, the white puffy clouds, and the brilliant sunshine are adding to our day's perfection.

"Francie, how about something cold to drink?"

"That sounds wonderful, Sean, since I'm parched," I respond.

"There is a guy selling drinks over there, Francie. I will be right back. Why don't you get us a spot there under the big tree, and we can have our picnic lunch over there?"

I take the sack lunches and find a small grass area. While I'm walking near the tree, I feel the cool breeze from the water while the white seagulls fly overhead. My hair is blowing under the cool shade of this mighty oak that must have been here for many years. Sean, smiling, sits down and hands me a soda.

"The root beer tastes wonderful, Sean."

"Let me try this sandwich you made, Francie. I'm starving. This melon is great, too. What a wonderful lunch! I'm having so much fun today."

"It is so entertaining to watch all the different people walking around, speaking their own languages from their faraway countries. You know, Sean, I wish our grandparents could have seen the beautiful lady as their ships sailed through the harbor past Bedloe Island."

"I was thinking the same thing, Francie. She still will be here, welcoming the newcomers that will be arriving all the time. The new immigrants will represent all those that never got a chance to see the Statue of Liberty in person. At least we get to see her, too."

After sitting and talking for a while, I feel as though I could just stay here in the shade all afternoon. Children are running freely in the exhilaration of the moment while the crowd is cheering joyfully. The band is beginning to play and is now starting with their first song, "When Johnny Comes Marching Home." It's a great inspirational Civil War song that is really a march that my grandfather probably listened to a long time ago.

Now they are playing "God Bless America." As everyone sings along, goosebumps go up and down my spine, and I get a shiver. The band looks stunning with their bright red-and-blue uniforms.

"It's really too bad that we have to leave before they are finished assembling the Lady," remarks Sean. "It has been so much fun! These are memories we will never forget, and it's so special because I am here with you, Francie!"

Of course, I am now smiling from ear to ear. I feel my face turning red and warm.

"Yes, Sean, I feel the same way. You have made this special occasion amazing for me also. It is a day I will never forget as well."

We just sit for a moment, looking into each other's eyes, not saying a word. Finally, Sean looks at his watch and sadly stands up first. He takes my hand in his and helps me up as it is time for us to leave. I take one final gaze at all the crowd and the ship and the large parts of the statue still lying on the dock next to the blue water. I want to imprint this perfect occasion forever in my memory. I am so thankful for the chance to have been here in this place and time with Sean.

We walk hand in hand to get on the ferry. As we climb up the steps to go back to the Jersey shore, the wind is much more blustery now, and the waves are splashing into the boat. We sway as the ship's horn blares loudly as we leave the harbor. I take Sean's arm and lean my head on his broad shoulder as we sit on the old chairs in the corner of the upper deck.

As the sun beats down and reflects off the water, I feel my face toasting in its rays. I can taste the sea salt spraying on my lips, and I feel the cooling water splashing all over me. The waves seem to be going higher and higher. I can't help but laugh as now we are soaking wet. We have had a magical day together.

When we get to the dock, Sean notices that the trolley is already filled. "Francie, we have to walk back."

"It will be lovely to take a walk. The trolley is so crowded anyway," I respond.

"Even the walkway is congested," I added.

"I can't believe there are so many people out and about, enjoying this glorious day," I remark. "I had the most wonderful time, Sean, but now I need to get over to Mrs. Ryan's house to take care of her kids."

I give him a hug and a kiss on his cheek, and while holding me tightly, Sean kisses me.

"I had a great day, too, Francie," Sean responds with a wide smile on his sunburned face. "I need to get back to the store. It was so nice of Mr. O'Malley to let me have time off today. Goodbye, Francie. Thanks for the great time. Those crates certainly aren't going to get unloaded by themselves, that's for sure!"

Sean is now walking in the opposite direction, and I feel so bad that our afternoon was cut so short. It seems like I always have to do the right thing and leave right in the middle of all the fun. I never get to spend a leisurely day relaxing during my summer vacation. We are forever rushing about from here to there, getting bits and pieces of enjoyment and relaxation in between all our never-ending responsibilities. I wonder if my life will ever change.

It's difficult for me to say goodbye to Sean, but now I have to hurry so I won't be late getting to Mrs. Ryan's house. Because of her "delicate" condition, she has a doctor's appointment later today. I will watch Eddie, her five-year-old, who is Austin's good chum, and her two-year-old, Danny. Mother says I need to be there for Mrs. Ryan since Mr. Ryan works all the time and she is expecting a baby in December.

Working for Mrs. Ryan is a part-time job for me, which I do appreciate since I can earn extra money to help our family. So I am now walking quickly through all the people who are out today. Since I am on a mission, I am trying to force a smile. A smile always brightens my mood.

Chapter 4

Everyone I pass as I walk through the crowded streets seems to be in such high spirits today. Strangers are greeting one another with a smile and a hello. I am also noticing that when I go anywhere, I see a lot more folks around town. Our city seems to be growing all the time. I guess they come to our community for the factory jobs. That is true with a lot of the urban areas, such as New York and Boston. In our city, workers in those plants here make purses, shoes, and a lot of other things, such as iron here in Newark.

Many newcomers also come because they have family in the city. So many of the Irish are here because their relatives live in Newark and family is so important. There are other ethnic groups in town, such as Germans, Italians, and Syrians, and blacks . They all have their own neighborhoods with their families. They must have come here for job opportunities, too. You do hear a lot of different languages spoken while you walk down the streets of Newark. It's nice to see all kinds of individuals in our section of the city. They seem to have their own ways of doing things, and it's nice that we all seem to get along mostly.

Today, with the arrival of the Lady Liberty, we are just one grateful melting pot—a mixture of races, religions, and cultures all glad to be here. I am in such a fine mood, thinking about our lovely morning.

I can't believe that I am here already at the Ryans. I stop for a minute and admire their pretty house. As I walk up the front porch steps of their white Cape Cod home, I notice the bright-blue shutters framing the long windows above the large stoop. Red and white geraniums line the walkway. I just love this place; it is so charming, especially with the big swing in the corner of the porch. Walking up to the front door, I hear nothing but unusual silence from the house. I gently knock, and Eddie comes running to meet me.

"Hurry up, Francie! You have to come upstairs," he demands.

I'm thinking, *Now what is going on?*

I rush up the stairway and see Mrs. Ryan in the boys' bedroom. As she's cradling the baby gently in her arms, he is whimpering.

"Francie, I am so glad to see you!" she exclaims. "Danny woke up this morning with a terrible fever, and my husband left so early for work. The baby is burning up! Can you go get Dr. O'Gormon, please?" she pleads with a very worried look on her face.

I immediately sprint down the stairway through the front door and off the porch, the screen door slamming behind me. It takes me a while though as I'm running as fast as I can while maneuvering quickly through the avenue. I race through the area of Newark known as Down Neck, where I can't help breathing in the fumes from the iron factories as I run to the doctor's office.

I begin to cough since my throat is very dry. There is his sign resting in front of the old red brick building. Luckily, the doctor is in his office as I can see him through the window, sitting at his desk, reading a huge book. I quickly knock as hard as I can on the large wooden door, and he lets me into his office.

"Dr. O'Gormon, you have to come quick! Little Danny Ryan is really sick. His temperature is awfully high."

As he picks up his doctor's bag, he says nothing, and we both dash down the street. In a few blocks, we are in front of St. James Church. The doctor stops suddenly in his tracks, pausing with a quick reverent bow of his head, and of course, I do the same. Then we are again on our way. In a little while, we are on the porch steps and into the house. We follow the sound of a screaming baby up the stairs to the far bedroom. Danny is lying on his parents' big bed, completely covered with a quilt and sweating terribly.

"Take these blankets and pajamas off the boy, Mrs. Ryan," orders Dr. O'Gormon. Then he looks at me. "I need a tub of cool water and some towels."

I hurry down to the kitchen, following the doctor's orders. When I come back upstairs, I see Danny's skin is a bright red; he also seems to be having lots of difficulty breathing. Mrs. Ryan covers the child with wet towels, trying to bring down his temperature. The doctor then takes out a bottle of rubbing alcohol from his old black bag and begins rubbing it onto Danny's little arms, legs, and back. While he does this a second time, Dr. O'Gormon's eyes are sadly looking at the boy's mother, who is now crying. Mrs. Ryan is very fearful, her hands are shaking.

"Mrs. Ryan, the baby has a high temperature of 105 degrees! Keep changing these cool cloths every half hour or so to help bring down his fever. Also, place a wet face cloth on his forehead. I will be back soon." He looks at me and back again at Mrs. Ryan. "You know, Mrs. Ryan, this is very serious," the doctor adds with a direct stare into her eyes. "There have been a lot of children in the neighborhood getting very ill with high fevers and flu."

She looks at me while taking a deep breath, trying to muster up all her strength and courage and trying not to become too emotional. I am doing my best to hold back tears.

"Francie, go get Father Donovan at St. James Church. Hurry! Danny needs his blessings!" Mrs. Ryan demands.

As I'm running out the screen door again, I am halfway down the street before I hear it slam this time. In a few minutes, I am knocking at the door of the rectory, which is next door to the church. Mrs. McGuire, the housekeeper opens the door, and I tell her of our emergency. She is very tall and her gray hair is put neatly in a bun. She greets us with a kind smile, then hurriedly turns to get the priest. Shortly after, Father Donovan finally comes running outside with a small black bag. Soon we are back at the house and up the stairs.

Immediately, Father Donovan removes a long purple stole from the bag, kisses it, and places it around his neck, with each part of the cloth dangling down his shoulders. He also retrieves the holy oil from his bag and begins placing some of the oil on the baby's forehead and the palms of his little hands. We all begin to pray with him.

Mrs. Ryan is now sobbing. I'm holding Eddie's hand, and he and I begin crying, too. Since the priest is giving Danny his last rites, we are all very sad and so scared. When he completes his litany, Father Donovan says a kind word and is on his way. Little Danny's face is flushed and feels extremely hot to the touch. Mrs. Ryan looks very tired, like she hasn't slept all night.

"Mrs. Ryan, I want to help you today. Why don't you sit and put your feet up and rest awhile?" I plead.

Saying nothing, she sits down in the rocking chair next to her bed, where little Danny is now fast asleep. After seeing that her boy is finally resting, Mrs. Ryan puts her head back and closes her eyes. In a minute, she's asleep.

When I was reading news articles with Sean yesterday, I read an interesting piece by Dr. Joseph Lister, who is a professor of surgery in London. He is the head of all the hospitals there. In his article, he thanks Dr. Louis Pasteur for his study on bacteria and how germs cause diseases. Since that research done by Dr. Pasteur, Dr. Lister instructs surgeons in the hospitals in England to wash their hands thoroughly before and after touching patients. Wounds and doctors' instruments are also cleaned thoroughly.

In English hospitals before Pasteur's study, they didn't even have sinks for the medical staff to wash. They thought just airing out the hospital once a day was enough to kill germs. More people will survive surgery now because patients' wounds are cleansed before their operations and the hospitals are also much more sterile.

It is also very interesting that Lister's father was a wine merchant who followed Pasteur's directions to boil wine quickly at a certain degree to kill the microbes that were spoiling the beverages of their time. They also boil milk to kill bacteria at a high temperature. Since this remedy was thought of by Dr. Pasteur, it is called pasteurization, and through his discovery and his work, milk is now much more healthy to drink. This Dr. Pasteur must be quite a scientist.

With all that in mind, I feel I should do something to get rid of the germs or microbes in the house that may be causing little Danny's sickness. So that his illness doesn't spread to the rest of their family, I decide to get out the cider vinegar from the cupboard. I also remove a pail from under the kitchen sink, add some water with vinegar, and find some washrags. With the mixture, I begin cleaning all the surfaces in the kitchen. I scrub the table, the floor, and the outside of the icebox. Now the house smells of strong vinegar, but at least it's clean. I quickly move to the baby's room, getting all his dirty laundry to wash.

"Come on, Eddie. Help me change the baby's crib. Do you know where your mother keeps the clean sheets and blankets?"

"They are here, Francie," he says as he walks to the closet in the upstairs hallway.

"I'm going to wash the crib and mattress before I put on the clean crib sheet." I grab the baby's soiled bedding to wash later. "Thank you so much for your help, Eddie. Why don't we wash up, and I will fix you some lunch after we make the baby's bed. There is ham and cabbage leftover in the icebox."

I warm the food and pour Eddie a glass of cold milk. There is a loaf of soft bread in the bread box, so I cut off a big piece.

"I'm sure little Danny will be feeling better soon," I say while Eddie devours his lunch. The poor boy is starving.

"Can I play with Austin later today?" he asks while taking a huge gulp of milk, which leaves a faint white mustache above his lips.

"Maybe he can come over later."

As I put the milk back in the icebox, I notice a whole cut-up chicken sitting in a metal pan. I take out an iron pot and begin making some chicken broth for the baby.

First, I brown the meat in hot oil. Next, I dice onions and celery and then add some potatoes and carrots and a little seasoning of parsley, salt, a dash of pepper, and garlic for flavor. I am trying to make it just like the way Mother does it. This soup will help everyone in the family feel better, especially little Danny.

As I finish putting in the seasonings, I hear Dr. O'Gormon coming into the house, carrying his bag and also some sort of gadget.

"Come, Francie," he orders. "We need to put the steamer by the baby so he can breathe easier, and rub some more rubbing alcohol on him with this sponge."

The baby is still sleeping. We can hear him breathing heavily, and with each breath, we can see his little chest rise up and down rapidly. His skin is pale, and when the doctor examines his mouth, we see his bright-red throat. The baby then begins to whimper, and Mrs. Ryan awakens, quickly jumping up from the rocking chair.

"Doctor, is he any better?" she asks.

"I'm not really sure yet," he answers while placing the thermometer under the baby's arm. The doctor puts the steamer near the boy's head on the bed. Soon there is a warm cloud of mist permeating the room. He then places a cool cloth on Danny's forehead, and at that moment, the baby slowly opens his beautiful blue eyes.

After what seems like forever, we can hear that Danny's breathing is less laborious. Sobbing, Mrs. Ryan picks up her crying little one and puts him close to her as tears stream down her face. She begins rocking him in the chair slowly in her arms as she softly sings an Irish lullaby.

Over in Killarney,
Many years ago,
My mother sang a song to me
In tones so sweet and low:
Just a simple little ditty,
In her old good Irish way
And I'd give the world if I could hear
That song of hers today
Too-ra loo-ra, Too-ra loo-ra li
Too-ra loo-ra, Hush now don't you cry!
Too-ra loo-ra loo-ra, Too-ra loo-ra li
That's an Irish lullaby.

Hearing that song, the baby immediately stops crying and is now resting his head gently on his mother's shoulder. He places his little arm tightly around her neck while giving his mother the biggest smile. Little Danny looks so much better. What a relief! The baby is breathing easier now and is falling back to sleep in his mother's arms. Then gently, Mrs. Ryan slowly stands up, lays him on her bed, and kisses him softly on his adorable face.

"The baby's high fever has come down. Mrs. Ryan, we are out of the woods! When he awakens, give him plenty of water to drink, and feed him some of that sensational chicken soup I smell simmering on the stove!" directs Dr. O'Gormon.

"You have our thanks, Doctor O'Gormon. We appreciate all your help, and may God bless you," Mrs. Ryan says as he gets ready to leave once more. He gives a nod and quickly heads downstairs. He is smiling, and I am very sure he is gratified with his day's work.

"Oh, Francie, thanks so much for your help, too, my dear. I don't know what I would have done without you today! I am sorry I won't be able to pay you until next week, though, until Mr. Ryan gets paid," she remarks.

"Please don't worry about that, Mrs. Ryan. I am just relieved that Danny is doing so much better. I'm also so glad that I was here today to help you!"

"You have to stay and have supper with us. Please try some of the marvelous soup you made that smells so delicious," requests Mrs. Ryan.

And of course, I wait for dinner. It is gratifying that Mrs. Ryan is so happy as she puts the little guy in his high chair. We all sit down around the table and have a bowl of tasty soup. We are very thankful that little Danny is doing so well. Later, as I am walking slowly home, I see the beautiful sunset of orange and pink radiating brilliantly through the evening sky; I realize that this is a day I shall not soon forget.

The morning brought Sean and me to the city to see the spectacular Statue of Liberty with all its excitement. We had such a marvelous time together. Little did we know what the afternoon was going to bring to the Ryan family. I guess one never knows what the day will bring.

Chapter 5

When I arrive home from the Ryans', it is late, and the aroma of amazing corned beef and cabbage hits me as I step through the side door. Supper is finished, the kitchen is all spruced up, and the dishes have been all put away in the cupboard.

As I walk in, I see Mary sitting at the kitchen table. How lovely she looks! Her long black hair is now past her shoulders. With her blue eyes, she looks so much like our dad. Her round-rimmed glasses are hanging down the bridge of her nose as she is lost in her reading. The bright chandelier that hangs from the ceiling above the kitchen table sparkles so, allowing us to read way into the night. We are so lucky that Thomas Edison lived here in Newark before going on to Menlo Park, New Jersey. We got electric lights last summer, and so many places around here have lights now.

Mary is such a sweet girl; we've always been very close. It was so exciting when she was born; I've always been grateful that I have a little sister. We are best friends even though sometimes we do argue. That girl, for an eleven-year-old, is such a wonderful reader. Whenever she has a spare moment, I see her nose is always in a book.

"Hi, Francie. It seems like you have been gone forever today," she remarks.

I explain to her what happened at the Ryans' house.

"Yes, it has been the longest day, starting with great fun, then worry about little Danny, and finally, relief!"

"I am so glad that he is doing fine," she replies with a look of concern on her face. She has an expression of concern on her face. "How are you doing after such a day, Francie? You have had a lot of interesting experiences lately," she adds before I can even answer. "How was it like to see the Statue of Liberty?"

"It was absolutely amazing! They were putting her together right on the dock. You will have to see her sometime standing tall and beautiful in the harbor!" I exclaim.

"Maybe I can go with you another time, and we can see her together," Mary adds.

"That would be fun, for sure!"

"Francie, I just read a wonderful book about the March family, *Little Women*. It is so delightful, and it is set during the Civil War, so it is really interesting. Someday I would like to play the part of Jo in the story. She is nothing like her sisters and is so strong-willed and independent. She wants to be a writer one day. That would be so fun to play that part. It is such an entertaining adventure—and sad too."

"I love that book, too, Mary. I know you would be great for the role of Jo," I added.

"Have you eaten, Francie?" she asks thoughtfully.

"Yes, I had supper with the Ryans," I reply.

"Francie, in the fall, our seventh-grade class at school will be doing a play, and I would like to try out for the lead!"

"You should, and I know you would do a great job. Seventh grade has a lot more fun activities for kids, and you will really enjoy the coming school year."

"Francie, I promised Mrs. Connor I would babysit for her tomorrow so I need to go to bed now since I have to get up early."

"Good night, Mary. I will be going to bed soon myself."

As Mary goes to turn in for the night, I decide to get out my diary from the little desk in the parlor. I write in it so often that the cover is falling off the book. Of course, I have to begin describing my exciting morning filled with enthusiasm and exhilaration in the city.

Sean was so kind and caring. I think he is becoming more than just a good friend. Just the very thought of him makes me content and happy. I will always remember our glorious trip to New York Harbor. That short journey today makes me wonder what other things may be out there for me and my future.

The afternoon was the complete opposite of the morning's promise. I will also never forget the look on Mrs. Ryan's face when Danny was so sick and how relieved she was when he finally got better. I cannot believe that all those events could happen in just one day.

Finally, I'm getting drowsy now, so I will go to bed, knowing that I can sleep in tomorrow. I am so looking forward to a day where I don't have to work and I can do whatever I feel like doing. Just the thought of that independence helps me climb into bed, take a deep breath, close my eyes, and think of nothing but pleasant thoughts as I fall fast asleep.

I am sleeping so soundly that I really don't know where I am when I hear a loud, clamorous crash; it's like the ceiling is coming down!

What in the world? I wonder.

I run downstairs to see what has happened. In the kitchen, I see Aunt Molly sitting on the floor, covered with flour. Her straggly brown hair has suddenly become completely white. There is flour everywhere—on the counter, all over the stove, and even in the sink. She is also sitting on several broken eggs on the black and white square designs on the floor. Eggshells are everywhere; their yolks are coloring the linoleum a runny yellow.

With such a sight, I cannot help but burst into loud laughter. "Aunt Molly, what happened?"

"Since I have the day off today, I thought it would be nice to bake some breakfast treats for the family. When I grabbed the carton of eggs, I took a step and slipped on the floor. I ended on top of them," she explains. "As I was falling, I knocked over the flour, which went everywhere."

"Here, Aunt Molly, let me help you."

I grab her arm and help her to her feet. I've never really realized how short she actually is. I suddenly feel sorry for Aunt Molly. She looks so small and helpless, and with her flour-white hair, she is aging before my very eyes. I guess Daddy is right; she really isn't that bad. We both clean up the mess together, laughing.

After Aunt Molly goes into her room to freshen up, I begin peeling some apples. Afterward, she finishes cutting up the fruit and puts them in the pie dish over the dough she made and then covers it all with the most beautiful crust. With some dough left over, Aunt Molly magically makes some hot cross buns, which really are my favorite.

"Thanks so much for your help, my darlin'," says Aunt Molly. "I can't wait to eat the goodies."

Aunt Molly puts the coffee pot on the stove, and its welcoming aroma passes through the kitchen; I certainly have to have some coffee this morning. Even the bubbling whiff from the percolator is starting to get me going.

Austin comes sauntering through the kitchen while trying desperately to remove the sleep from his eyes. He looks so cute this morning with his red hair sticking up every which way. The auburn color contrasts with his blue and white nightshirt, which stretches down to his feet.

"I smell apples and cinnamon and good stuff coming from the oven!" he exclaims.

As Austin finds a chair to plop down on, I feel that this is the perfect time to warn him again about the dogs in the neighborhood because I must have seen at least thirty of them running wild when I walked home from Mrs. Ryan's house.

"Austin, I saw lots of dogs on my way home last night. It was kind of scary because some of them were barking really loud and walked very close while not taking their eyes off of me. I was afraid that some of them were really mean by the way they were acting."

"You already told me that, Francie. I am not a baby, and I can take care of myself," he says. "You don't need to worry about me."

I feel a cringe in my stomach. Sometimes, I have such a sense of helplessness. I don't seem to have control of anything in my life. I quickly sit down, and without thinking, I grab a hot bun but immediately drop it on the table; it had burned the palm of my hand. Right now, I am so nervous, but I feel Aunt Molly's baking will give me comfort. I wait a moment and then try the pastry. It is so luscious with the sweet, white icing all over the buns, and they taste so delectable with the coffee.

I am going to save a couple for Sean, as I know he will just love them. Aunt Molly can bake anything. We love everything she makes. She also bakes for the O'Brien household in Morristown, where she goes almost every day to work. With her making them fresh bread and desserts daily, they must appreciate Aunt Molly so much.

After I finish my coffee and a piece of the succulent apple pie, I decide to go for a long walk. Maybe the fresh air will help improve my mood. As I step outside by the front door, I see on the stoop a pamphlet explaining the upcoming festivities of the St. James Church's Fourth of July celebration. The festival notice has really gotten my attention, so I take a seat on the porch step and continue to browse.

There are all kinds of things for families to do this Fourth of July. In the morning, children can participate in races and games. The church is providing hot dogs, while each family can bring a dish to share. Reading further, I notice that there will be fireworks later in the evening. Also, there is an invitation for all those who play Irish music to come to the festivities and bring their instruments.

As I open the leaflet inside, I notice in very large letters the words "Pie-Baking Contest," inviting anyone who would wish to enter to compete for a blue ribbon. Suddenly, I have a great idea!

Of course, I have to run back into the apartment to show Aunt Molly. Back in the kitchen, I see Mother slowly sipping her steaming hot coffee while little Collin is sitting in his high chair, enjoying some apple pie, evidenced by little pieces of cooked apples on his plump cheeks. Aunt Molly finally sits down to enjoy some of her delicious baking.

"Aunt Molly, look what I found on the porch." As I show her the brochure, her brown eyes become very large.

There is such excitement in her voice as she responds, "Oh my!"

As I am laughing so loudly, it is very difficult for me to speak. "You make the best pies in the whole world, Aunt Molly! I bet you will win the blue ribbon."

"I know you can," joins in Mother. "What kind of pie would really impress the judges?"

Aunt Molly, while contemplating, answers, "I think a blueberry pie would be wonderful with fresh blueberries that are starting to come out now. Blueberry pie is definitely my specialty!"

Mother agrees, "I think that is great, Molly! That is really your best pie and quite pretty looking too. The judges will be so impressed!"

"I am going to have to practice my pie-baking skills on the Fitzgerald family, and you can let me know if there is anything I can improve on!" exclaims Aunt Molly.

I am so glad that my aunt finally has something to look forward to and not just working all the time. As little Collin is finished eating, I decide to take him with me on my walk. I clean him up and put on his little shorts, polo shirt, and matching blue hat; he looks so cute. I place him in his buggy, which all the Fitzgerald kids have used over the years.

It is such a gorgeous morning outside. The baby birds are chirping loudly in the robin's nest inside the crimson burning bush in front of the porch. We can stroll to the park, and Collin can see the ducks in the stream. As we walk toward the water, I can smell the fragrance of wild raspberries near the woods. I know how much Collin would love these red berries, so I stop to pick some. Suddenly, a sharp thorn stabs my finger, and it begins to bleed. The pain I am feeling and the red blood oozing out of my hand make me think immediately of that dead fox I seem to never forget.

We are not too far from the very spot where the animal was lying. As we continue our journey, I move more slowly, intently canvassing the area and making sure there are no wild animals close to my little brother. I pick up some rocks on our way just in case I see any scary creatures roaming.

Chapter 6

The Fourth of July will be here tomorrow, and I am wondering why the summer is racing by so quickly. All everyone has been talking about is the festival at St. James Church. Aunt Molly has been practicing her blueberry pies on us all week. Frankly, I am getting rather tired of blueberry pie; I sure hope she wins the contest after all the pie we have had to eat these last several days.

Cabbage, carrots, and green onions are collected on the kitchen table as Mother begins to make her tasty cabbage salad using her old standby of oil, vinegar, and lemon. My preferred medley is her potato salad, which she is also bringing to the picnic. The potatoes are boiled firmly, cooked to perfection, and seasoned with parsley, a dash of salt and pepper, oil, and a touch of lemon. She puts several eggs for added flavor. Her salads are so scrumptious, and I know everyone will love them both.

I thought I should bring something, too, so I am making chocolate cupcakes with chocolate frosting. I am also excited because Sean is meeting us there and chocolate is his very favorite.

"Well, thank you all for your wonderful help!" said Aunt Molly. "I have just finished my pie for the contest. I'm really getting nervous about the whole thing."

"Your pies are the very best," responds Daddy.

"We need to get there early this morning," reminds Austin. "The sack races start at nine. There will be foot races in the churchyard and a tug of war contest in the afternoon."

It is a cool Fourth of July morning as we all parade as a family up Lafayette Street to St. James Church. The old red brick building looks stately with the red roses surrounding the walkway. In the front yard stands an old Irish cross with a circle in its center, joining the old Celtic beliefs with our modern faith, which blends the old and the new. It is quite quaint and very different from other crosses you see on churches. I have never seen so many people at our church as I see today. The Gleasons from down the street are walking ahead of us, carrying a large picnic basket. As Austin sees his buddies, he takes off to the lot next to the church to take part in the races.

"We better hurry to the backyard so we can get a table," remarks Mother as we pick up speed while carrying all the food.

"Yes, Mama, there is one table left near the pie-tasting station," I quickly reply.

Aunt Molly nervously carries her beautifully crisscrossed, crusted pie with her trembling hands as she walks very slowly and carefully to the judges' booth in front of our table. I have never seen Aunt Molly so excited.

Mother places a red and white plaid tablecloth over the old, weathered picnic table. As we arrange our wonderful lunch, I see Sean carrying a large paper bag to our table.

"Hi, Francie, I brought some root beer. Mr. O'Malley gave me all these bottles for your family."

"That was so thoughtful of him, Sean," I said, smiling.

As we are all sitting at the table, watching all the families arriving at the festival, we can smell the hot dogs sizzling on the charcoal. I don't think there is a better aroma in the whole world than those frankfurters grilling. While we are patiently waiting to enjoy our meal, Mr. O'Connor, our next-door neighbor, has brought out his bagpipe and is now warming up to play. Of course, I love the beautiful, vibrant sound of a bagpipe, which is so much a part of our Irish culture. With the first melody, shivers go up and down my spine. Another neighbor brings out her fiddle to accompany him to "Yankee Doodle Dandy."

Now they are playing "My Darling Irish Rose" followed by some lovely Celtic music. Presently, so many are getting up inspired by our traditional songs and dancing the Irish way, lining up in long single rows. They are kicking their legs up and down, back and forth in unison without moving their straight arms, which they hold close to their sides.

We all begin to laugh as my sweet sister, Mary, joins the group. Sean is sitting close to me, holding my hand as he takes in the merriment. Of course, I have to grab his arm and pull him out as we begin dancing with the others. We are laughing so hard we can barely stand, so we decide to head back to our seats.

I am really enjoying myself as the sun's warmth shines on me as it moves from behind a fluffy, white cloud. I love the sun's rays in my face. By this time, Eddie and Austin, out of breath, come running up to our table.

"Francie, we got a ribbon for second place!" Austin excitedly remarks.

"Yeah, we got a ribbon for the sack races," adds Eddie.

"That is wonderful, especially since I noticed that you were some of the youngest kids out there," I remark. This is going to be a wonderful day of celebration. I just know it will be the best Fourth of July ever!

Mrs. Ryan stops at our table with little Danny in his buggy. "Good day," Mrs. Ryan says.

"Hi, Mrs. Ryan," I answer with a big bright smile as always, remembering the adventure we had together at her house. That day when Danny was so sick has helped us to connect as good friends forever.

I help her a few times a week with chores, and I also work in her huge yard, which constantly needs weeding and watering all summer. She has several tomato plants, beans, cucumbers, pumpkins, and even watermelons growing in her big beautiful backyard. She is always giving us some of her homegrown tomatoes, which are the tastiest. The Ryans also raise chickens in their backyard, so every week, she gives us several eggs, which are the freshest we have ever tasted.

"Please, Katie, come and sit down with us," directs Mother.

Mrs. Ryan has brought big ripe tomatoes, cucumbers, and onions in a large vegetable plate, which she places on the center of the table.

"Let's make room for Eddie too," says Mama. "He can sit next to Austin. How are you feeling these days, Katie?"

"I have been a little tired lately," replies Mrs. Ryan. "I am so glad to have Francie's help, that's for sure."

"Please have some lunch with us, Katie," invites Father. "I can't believe how big Danny is getting."

So Mrs. Ryan joins our party, also bringing out of her picnic basket several ears of corn that are still steaming. The butter she also brought melts quickly on the hot, golden ears. We can smell the fragrance of sweet steamed corn all over the yard. What a wonderful picnic it is!

We are enjoying the delicious salads, grilled hot dogs, and cold root beer. Soon Austin has devoured two ears of corn, while little Collin has spent several minutes in amazement, eating his first ear of corn ever, which he holds tightly between his two little hands. Mother first broke the large corn in half than cooled it for him, letting it sit in a cup with cold water. Now, he is intently concentrating on hanging on to the cob while enjoying every kernel, except for the little pieces that dot his face.

"What a grand day it is," remarks Mrs. Ryan. "It is not too hot, just perfect."

"We couldn't have picked a nicer day," remarks Aunt Molly.

My aunt has hardly touched her food. She keeps staring at the pie station as she slowly moves the potato salad gently around her plate. She looks as though she is contemplating whether she should eat or not. Finally, they are coming around the front of the table with the pies, putting them on display for all of us to admire.

Suddenly, we hear one of the judges asking for all the participants of the pie-baking contest to come forward. I can see Aunt Molly's lips are quivering as she quickly jumps up and shuffles as fast as can to the pies, which are now placed on the table in perfect order, tempting all. The pastries look so wonderful. How I would love to have just a morsel of each of them! Soon, a short heavy gentleman with a round black derby walks out of the pie-tasting tent.

"Ladies and gentlemen, may we have your attention, please," the judge announces. "We have our winners of the pie-baking contest. The third-place winner is Alva Anderson with her delicious traditional American apple pie. Next, the second-place winner is Janet Tillman, who delighted us with her succulent peach pie. And now we would like to present the first-place winner. The blueberry pie baked by Molly Murphy is the blue-ribbon winner of the contest. She has baked the perfect, flakiest crust and combined with the sweetest blueberries we have ever tasted."

The judge hands Aunt Molly the blue ribbon. The rest of the bakers walk back slowly to their seats disappointedly, with their shoulders drooping.

Aunt Molly is so thrilled. She is smiling and laughing as she accepts her award. When she comes back to our table, we are all standing and applauding. Tears are now falling down her face. She is so emotional that she cannot say anything, so at this point, she sits down while taking a purple hankie out of her big purse and tries drying her tears without ever letting go of her beautiful blue ribbon. I am so thrilled for my aunt!

"I told you that you make the best pies, Molly," Daddy says.

"I love anything you bake, Molly," Mother adds. "What is your secret?"

We wait patiently for Aunt Molly to get her composure as we take our seats at the table. Taking a deep breath and drinking some root beer, Aunt Molly begins to explain, "Well, it's always the small things in the making of a great pie, such as adding a little zest from a lemon peel to the blueberries mixed in with a little sugar. We also put the pie dough in the icebox for a short time to firm a while before adding the fruit. Our mother was such a great baker. I learned everything from her. Baking is really just a labor of love. If we want to do anything well, we have to put our whole heart and joy in it."

Everyone is having such a great time. What a wonderful way to celebrate our country's birthday. Tonight there will be fireworks we can see across the river. Presently, they are putting more hot dogs on the grill which smell so appetizing. We are contemplating trying some of those delightful pies that are sitting so close that we can almost taste them.

As we are sitting, we are shocked to see out of nowhere a pack of wild, stray dogs charging for the meat on the grill. Ladies scream, while the men stand up, not really knowing what to do next. Not very far behind is a police officer in hot pursuit. Then without warning, the table with the pies is suddenly flipped over by two large yelping dogs who take a moment to sniff the succulent pastries. The marvelous pies we have been eyeing are now strewn everywhere. The hounds continue running in a single file as a policeman runs after them with a pistol in his hand.

Aunt Molly lets out the most awful scream as she sees her award-winning pie turned upside down in the dirt and begins sobbing uncontrollably into her hankie. Now I am again suddenly reminded of the fox lying dead in the brush; I am more frightened than ever! Sean can tell I am upset, so he takes my hand in his and says nothing. Nobody says anything for what seems like an eternity.

Chapter 7

Sean and I decide to go for a long walk since we finally have a day off together. Later, we will stop at O'Leary's Drugstore, where they sell the best chocolate sodas in the whole world! They combine the most delicious chocolate-and-vanilla ice cream mixed with iced soda, making the most scrumptious and satisfying treat. To top it all off, they add two sweet cherries over lots of whipped cream.

As we walk hand in hand through the park, I smell the traditional summer scent of freshly cut grass. The air is cooling as we slowly stroll near the tall blue evergreens near the lake. Their branches are sparkling in the morning sun. I can't believe how happy I am this morning. The simple things in life can help us be so content. On our way up the hill, we stop to graze at the scarlet roses damp with the morning dew, giving off such a lovely fragrance.

As I get closer and closer to the flowers, I suddenly hear a deafening buzzing sound.. I look around, not knowing where the noise is coming from. Abruptly, Sean grabs both my shoulders and pulls me quickly away as a multitude of bees are flying out of their hive in the tree above me. My goodness! The swarm is coming right at me!

Sean screams, "Run, Francie, run!"

"Ahh!" I yell as Sean grabs my hand.

We race as fast as we can down the hill, away from the flowers. Finally, we are safe in the meadow. I'm trying desperately to catch my breath as we now slow down.

"That was a close one, Francie!"

"That was quick thinking Sean. There were so many bees coming out of that hive. It was scary."

"With beautiful blossoms, there will be lots of bees nearby," he explains.

"Sean, look at those two mourning doves on the branch over there on the large elm tree," I say, drawing his attention.

"My mother always calls them love doves because they always seem to be in pairs, Francie," as Sean says as he again takes my hand, smiling. Of course, I have to smile, as I am now turning beet red.

I can see O'Leary's in the distance; we are almost there, finally. I'm so looking forward to that cold soda now. As we walk closer, I can see the paint is peeling on the old building. The steps going to the porch creak loudly as we go up. Then Sean grabs the door. As we step inside the store, we notice a *New York World* sitting on a newspaper rack next to the entrance. Standing in disbelief, Sean looks at me, and I look at him. We stare once again down at the newspaper headlines. We see the surprising title and once more look at each other, not believing what we are reading. *Can this possibly be true?*

In bold black letters, the headline shouts: "BOY WITH RABIES CURED BY DR. LOUIS PASTEUR IN PARIS."

Sean quickly takes out a nickel from his pocket and buys a copy of the newspaper. As we sit down at the lunch counter, we are in complete awe as we read the following intriguing article:

Joseph Meister, nine, of Alsace, France, was badly bitten by a rabid dog on July 4 at 1:00 p.m. The dog had thrown the boy down on the ground and bit him fourteen times on his hands, thighs, and legs before escaping. The mongrel was later killed by its owner. Dr. Webber, Joseph Meister's family doctor, concurred the dog had rabies because it had been viciously growling and foaming at the mouth. When the doctor examined the dead canine, he also found unusual things in the dog's stomach, such as hay and wood, which are things rabid animals eat.

Since Joseph's wounds were festering, Dr. Webber suggested that the Meisters, as soon as possible, take Joseph to Dr. Louis Pasteur. Two days later, Joseph, his mother, and a family friend arrived in Paris by train. After examining his wounds, Dr. Pasteur concurred that if the boy was not given the vaccine soon, he most likely would die a terrible death from rabies.

At 8:00 p.m. on July 6, Dr. Grancher, Dr. Pasteur's colleague, began giving the boy the first of his shots under the skin of his stomach. The vaccine was made from a small piece of a spinal cord from a rabbit that had died of rabies. His first injections were made of diseased spinal cords that were two weeks old and were much weaker in strength. As the daily shots progressed, they were becoming increasingly strong since those vaccines were taken from a much more recently deceased animal's spinal cord.

By the time the shots were given on July 16, a one-day-old spinal cord injection was used, which was the strongest vaccine yet. By slowly increasing the dosage, Joseph's body gradually fought off the disease and on July 28, Joseph finally went home with his mother to Alsace, cured.

For several minutes, Sean and I don't say anything; we are just contemplating what we have just read. There are all kinds of thoughts rushing through my mind. Of course, my thoughts go back to the dead fox by the brush.

"Francie, I can't believe that Dr. Pasteur has developed a cure for rabies!" Sean brings me back to the present.

"Sean, while we were celebrating the Fourth of July in Newark, poor Joseph Meister was being brutally attacked by a rabid dog in France. He suffered so much, but now can you believe that there is a remedy for such an awful disease?"

"Francie, this is a first! It is as though it was meant for us to come here today and find out about the good news about Joseph Meister."

"What fate is this?" I ask.

I am here in a drugstore in Newark, staring at a photograph of Dr. Louis Pasteur, which is also on the front page of today's newspaper. I see his chiseled features and his serious deep-set deep-set, dark eyes looking out at the world he serves. What kind of man is this? It would be really something to meet him someday. Although that vision of the dead animal near the woods never completely leaves my mind, but suddenly, I am not as fearful as I was that terrifying morning. Hopefully, life as we know it is changing for the better.

"Isn't that incredible, girl!"

"That makes me feel a lot better about everything, Sean."

"I knew it would." Sean smiles. "So people can be treated after being bitten by a rabid animal with a series of shots, and they can survive from the disease. That is a miracle! For years, when someone is attacked by a diseased animal, doctors would cauterize or burn the infected area with a branding iron and just hope for the best. The whole neighborhood could hear those victims screaming in agony during the process. Those poor wretched souls," Sean adds.

We sit at the counter for quite a while, finishing our cool beverages, thinking about what the great Dr. Pasteur has been able to accomplish. Sean is now in deep thought as he stares out the store window. After a while, he takes a deep sigh and grabs the paper and is now leafing through it until he finds his favorite part, of course, the sports section. Sean loves to read about all the games, and while he catches up on all the scores, I am slurping what is left of my drink. After reading about Joseph Meister, it seems as though a heavy load has been lifted off my shoulders.

"Francie, the New York Mets are tied for first place, and they are playing at home today. Why don't we see the game this afternoon?"

"Since I am in the best mood I have been in quite a long time, that sounds like a great idea, Sean. I would love to go. New York now has the Metropolitan Opera House and the Metropolitan Museum of Art and our very own favorite Metropolitan baseball team," I explain.

With a big smile, Sean advises, "Francie, we better get going if we are to make the game by one o'clock in New York."

As we leave O'Leary's, we grab today's newspaper, making sure we don't leave our important article.

"It is so nice out today. Why don't we walk to the ferry?" I suggest.

We are finally going to see the New York Metropolitans play. We have not had a chance to go to a game all summer. They are our favorite professional baseball team and doing quite well this year. As we were walking to the boat, I am appreciating that both Sean and I are finally getting some time together. We are again taking the ferry into New York, reminding me of our last exciting trip into the city.

I recall the fun we had that delightful day when we went to see the Statue of Liberty when she had just arrived at our shores. There in front of us, we see her once again, but now she is standing tall with her arm raised high with a torch in hand. The Lady stands magnificently on her pedestal, which is firmly placed in the harbor for all of us to see.

The blue sea appears calm as the boat glides through the water. It is so peaceful from our vantage point high on the ferry's upper deck. Today, the sea symbolizes my serene disposition. I am so relaxed sitting next to Sean that before I know it, we have arrived in the city. Getting off the craft and on to the shore, we feel a warm summer breeze as we stroll to the polo grounds. I guess a lot of people have the same idea this beautiful day as there are hundreds here as we walk quickly into the ballpark.

The big arena is in front of us as we step through the gate. Sean buys our tickets as we enter the stadium, and since it is Ladies' Day today, I get in for half the price. Sean is also buying a program to keep up with all the players who are in the game. As we see the participants throwing the ball around, we hurry to our seats. I notice how white our home team's uniforms are against the backdrop of a vivid emerald field. The white first base and third base chalk lines also contrast with the green grass, making the ballpark even more spectacular.

Luckily, we have excellent seats in the upper deck, looking down at the left field. John O'Rourke is playing left field today, and he is right under our upper-deck vantage point. We will get to see all the great catches he makes this afternoon.

"Who is pitching?" I ask.

"Tim O'Keefe. He has won fifteen games already this year," boasts Sean.

As the game is getting ready to begin, we stand respectfully for the singing of our national anthem. The stadium is now completely hushed; it is almost like being in church. This is the only time in the game that this park will be so still and silent. Before the anthem begins, men are taking off their hats and placing them over their hearts reverently as they stand tall, facing our striking red, white, and blue American flag.

We are observing our nation's banner, which is now blowing beautifully in a bold breeze in the direction where we are sitting in the left-field bleachers. When the "Star-Spangled Banner" is complete, Tim O'Keefe throws out the first pitch to the starting lineup of the Baltimore Orioles, and the game begins.

The fans are cheering, and I hear vendors saying, "Get your red hots! Get your peanuts! Get your popcorn!"

As the men walk by with those delightful treats, there is the heavenly aroma of popcorn and melted butter and steaming red hots, so Sean and I have to indulge because you can't go to a ball game without having one of the best-tasting hot dogs in the world. These frankfurters are seasoned to a spicy perfection and placed in a delicious soft bun.

Since we are sitting directly in the hot sun without any shade, Sean buys some cold sodas also. There are vendors walking around, selling souvenirs, which include pennants, little wooden baseball bats, and large pencils with the team logo. They are kind of expensive, so we decide not to buy anything; just remembering today is our best souvenir.

I am really enjoying the game. We have scored a couple of runs; the Orioles are leading by one, but in baseball, anything can happen and usually does. That is why baseball is America's favorite pastime. The game is going by very quickly, and this is so much fun that I don't want the festivities to ever end. In fact, I am praying for a slight rain delay, but with this stunning sunshine, that's not going to happen today.

We are already at the bottom of the ninth inning. The Metropolitans are behind the Orioles by one run, Baltimore has 3, New York has 2. Our team is now up to bat. Ed Kennedy, the first baseman, hits the ball in the outfield out past the third baseline. Kennedy makes it to second base, but the umpire calls the hit a foul ball, and Kennedy has to come back again to bat.

Jim Muntrie, the Mets' manager, comes running out, screaming at the umpire, and the Metropolitans' first-base coach joins the manager in the shouting match. Now they are both screaming in the umpire's face. Before you know it, it's a donnybrook, and both teams are yelling and kicking dirt on each other's shoes.

There are several players yelling at the top of their lungs on the field. Since both the managers will not calm down, Jim Muntrie and the first base coach are both kicked out of the game.

After that, all the other players are back to their positions, and the game resumes.

"We are really getting our money's worth of entertainment today." Sean laughs.

After all that, Kennedy then strikes out. Now the crowd is really booing. There is one out, and Steve Brady is next to bat for the Metropolitans' home team. He drives a single to left field. The New Yorkers now have one on first base and one out. John O'Rourke is up to bat next. He is a left-hander facing the right-handed pitcher of the Orioles, Mike Martino. Martino looks at the runner on first base, keeping him close to the bag so Brady doesn't steal second base.

Now the pitcher fires a fastball high over the plate. O'Rourke powerfully swings at the first pitch and we know immediately when the bat hits the ball that it will be out of the park. The speeding white sphere soars toward us in the left-field bleachers over the home run fence. It is a magnificent home run.

Sean does not take his eyes off the baseball, which is now coming directly at him. Suddenly, he leaps up, extending his long arm as high as he can, knocking the ball down and catching it with his right hand. He drops it out of his right hand and then scoops it up with his left. The ball now is going from one hand to the other, bobbling back and forth, until finally, Sean manages to catch it with both hands together.

With a wide grin, he hands the ball to me and says, "Here, my dear; your souvenir for this lovely day!"

"Thank you very much," I reply, laughing so hard I can hardly stand. We both begin cheering as loud as we can!

As I take the bruised leather ball from Sean, I can't help but give him a kiss on his lips. He then puts his arms around me, and I hold him ever so tightly, not ever wanting to let go of his tender embrace. After that home run, though, we have to savor the moment since fans are going absolutely wild; there is pandemonium in the park! Everyone is screaming and jumping up and down, and now so are we.

At this point in time, I am, without a doubt, the happiest girl around. I am happy that the Metropolitans have won and are now back in first place by themselves and that I am at the game with Sean, who is now more than my best friend. He is my boyfriend.

Chapter 8

The summer is flying by, and even though it is still very warm outside, the time for fun is passing. School will be here before we know it. I am so excited to be attending Newark High School. It is a dream that I have had for a very long time. Francie Fitzgerald will be the first girl in our family to get a higher education! Furthering my schooling will help me to get on with my life outside of the tenements of Newark, New Jersey.

I am also so happy to be walking to and from school with Sean. It is nice to have an upperclassman show me the ropes. Later today, Sean and I are going to go to the high school so I can look around and see everything for the first time.

As excited as I am to go back to school, Austin is definitely not looking forward to ending his summer vacation. He is thrilled to go to school this year as much as he would love to have calves liver and onions for supper tonight. Mother took him over to see his new class yesterday at St. James School, and since Austin saw his name on the door of Sister Mary Alice's classroom, he has been upset ever since. Having heard all the awful stories, he is petrified to be one of her students. I completely understand his frame of mind since she was my third-grade teacher, too. Her teaching methods are way too strict for little kids Austin's age.

Mother took him shopping for school clothes yesterday afternoon, which did not improve his mood in the slightest. His outfits consist of two pairs of blue pants and two white short-sleeve shirts he will be wearing to start the school year. Even with his little frown this morning, he is still as cute as he always is, with his messy red hair sticking in every direction. His matching freckles all over his face, and his reddish skin tone from all those summer days in the sun make him look adorable.

Mary is sitting at the kitchen table, finishing her breakfast of oatmeal and berries. I decide to join her since the aroma is so inviting and I am so hungry.

"I am so looking forward to going into the seventh grade, Francie," Mary says as she eats every morsel in the bowl.

"Mary, I enjoyed being in the seventh grade. That's when I started to like learning. Even though you are young, it is never too early to start thinking about those things you may want to study and do in life. School is going to be more fun and challenging since you can now try out for the student government and do other fun things. Of course, you know you can start playing against other schools in sports. Won't that be exciting?"

"Yes, Francie! I guess the Fitzgerald girls are ready for the new school year to begin!"

"I guess we are, Mary. I feel bad for Austin, though. I know he will eventually adjust to his new classes, but I can't help but chuckle at his fate."

"I know! I feel sorry for him, too."

As I finish my hot breakfast, I am starting to get enthusiastic about going to Newark High School.

"Mary, Sean is going to be showing me my new school later."

"How exciting! Someday I will be going to high school, and I look forward to it."

"It's fun, Mary, and I am so happy I am finally at this stage of my life. You will get there before you know it. Just work hard and keep those grades up."

I am cleaning up the breakfast dishes as Mother comes into the kitchen, carrying little Collin, whom she puts in his high chair. I give the baby a kiss and give Mama a hug before leaving. I can't believe how much taller I am getting than Mother.

"Mama, I'm going to wait outside for Sean."

"Sure, honey," she replies. "I think it is a great idea for you to visit your new school before you start your classes, Francie."

I take my usual spot on the porch step as I wait for Sean. Eddie Ryan, Patsy Reynolds, and my little brother Austin are playing tag on the lawn. Since Austin is "it," he is chasing little

Eddie around the front yard, and Eddie is scurrying away as fast as his little legs can carry him. I really can't stop laughing!

Then something catches my eye, and I can't believe what I am seeing! Is this my imagination? I grasp the awful revelation of three big, black dogs galloping after the boys down the block. All of a sudden, I feel so scared that my outreached hands are shaking. Now in hot pursuit following the barking dogs are two policemen. As they get closer to the boys, I can see the huge Labrador in the lead is foaming at the mouth and his glossy eyes are glaring at Austin.

I am suddenly off the porch and on the lawn. That hideous brute is snarling and growling while displaying his ugly, sharp teeth. The police officer draws his pistol out of his holster and, with one eye closed, aims it directly at the vicious animal that is now panting in my brother's face.

With all the courage I can muster, I scream as loud as I can, "Boys, get up on the stoop *now*!"

The boys make a mad dash to the porch. The policeman fires two quick deafening shots. We hear a yelp, and then we know this poor creature has been put out of its misery. The other dogs in the group race away. I not only see the bleeding dog there on the sidewalk in front of us but also my dreadful flashback to that awful morning at the lake that began my terrifying dream I seem to be living. With the sound of the gunshot, a crowd starts forming in front of our apartment.

Presently, I see Sean bolting up Union Street. "I can't believe what just happened!" Sean exclaims. "That was a close one, Francie! Is everybody all right?"

"Yes, Sean, we're okay," I answer. "Thank goodness the policeman was here to finish him. Those sick dogs are so scary. They can attack at any time!"

"Okay, everybody, you need to go back about your business," orders the officer to what has now become a large cluster of neighbors standing on our front lawn. The policeman is slowly placing the gun back in its holster. Mother is now on the porch, holding Collin tightly in her arms while letting the door slam.

"They really need to do something about these crazy dogs that run freely all hours of the night and day around here," Mother explains, her voice quivering. I hate to see Mother so upset. Her face is flushed, and she is breathing heavily with the look of fear in her eyes.

The children and I are now huddled closely together on the porch, feeling safe in one another's presence. Sitting here altogether, we try desperately to catch our breath. Everyone is quiet except for little Eddie, who is crying uncontrollably. I hold him tightly as I put him gently on my knee, kissing him ever so softly on his cheek.

"Everything is okay, Eddie," I say as I try to remain calm.

"That dog was growling at me, Francie," explains Austin.

As I see the fear in my brother's eyes, I begin to cry.

What a disappointing morning! Now I really don't feel like going anywhere. I slowly get up to go back inside the house after giving Sean little Eddie. I try to comfort Mama as I put my arm around her shoulder and escort her back into the apartment. A glass of cold water should help me try to gain a little composure. I don't think my life will ever be the same since my old horror has reclaimed me once again.

I hear Sean calling me, and I know we have to go. I take a deep breath and force a smile as I walk out the door. I take his strong hand into mine, and Sean and I start to stroll slowly down Union Street. The scary encounter has put a damper on my mood, but time is marching on and before we know it, school will be starting.

On our way, I suddenly notice every detail. There is a huge red maple on the corner that must have been here for many years. It is so stately and majestic in the sunlight, and its leaves are moving ever so slightly in a soft breeze. We see children romping outside, enjoying their last days of summer vacation. Before we know it, Sean and I are on the corner of Washington and Linden Streets, and right in front of us is the new and impressive Newark High School.

My heart beats rapidly as I sprint up the steps of the brilliant red brick building. Sean has to hurry to catch me.

"Here we are, Francie. Here at last is your beautiful new school!"

I can hardly believe that I am finally here. Sean opens the big wooden door, and I slowly enter this splendid building. My heart is pounding with excitement. Big round, light fixtures hang from a perfect white ceiling. The scent of the familiar fragrance of floor wax hits me as we walk in on the gleaming new tile. The school is huge compared to St. James and so are the drinking fountains which lean against the light-green walls. And now, finally, I can take a deep breath and inhale; the school has such a calming effect. Here is where I belong! This is what I have always dreamed about.

There are lots of other students walking around, exploring the school, also. Sean recommends that I pick up a copy of my schedule so I can find out where my classes are. Walking into the large office, the anticipation overwhelms me.

"Hello," I say as I anxiously greet the secretary. "I would please like to see a copy of my schedule. My name is Frances Fitzgerald, and I am a new ninth-grader this year." I see her name on the large plaque on her shiny, oak desk.

Mrs. Morgan looks through a small metal file case on the counter and finds my name. As she hands me my schedule, smiling, she says, "Here you go, my dear, and you can keep this copy for your use." I quickly take it from her, not meaning to grab it out of her hand.

"Thank you, Mrs. Morgan."

"Let me see. I am taking rhetoric, Latin, algebra, reading and writing, vocal music, and science." As I read, my voice cracks. I can see that I will have a full load this semester; it really looks like a great deal of homework. Sean can tell I am a little nervous about all the classes I will need to take.

"These are good subjects, Francie. You will do fine. I know you are up to the challenge," he adds. "Let's start looking around. We should go upstairs since most of your classes are on the second floor."

Going up the stairs, I realize that this is a really big school, and as we get to the second floor, we see Room 206. Miss O'Grady is at her desk.

"She is a very good teacher. I had her last year," Sean whispers as we walk into her room.

She is wearing wire-rimmed glasses, which droop below the bridge of her nose and is sitting behind so many books and papers we can barely see her. Her hair is jet-black and is rolled on the top of her head. While she is reading intently, I notice that the new wooden desks in her classroom are in perfect order, with each displaying a round inkwell in their right corners of the desks, inviting me to sit down right now and join her class.

Finally, Miss O'Grady notices us. "Welcome," she says, waking me from my vision.

"Hello, I am Francie Fitzgerald, and I am going to be in your second-hour class."

"Welcome, Francie. I am Miss O'Grady, and I am very glad to meet you. Hi, Sean, how has your summer been?"

"It went by much too quickly, Miss O'Grady, since I have been way too busy working," answers Sean.

I notice the room is so pleasing and colorful. There is a lovely pattern of rust and green leaves alternating around the border of each of the two bulletin boards in the back of the room. The sun is shining brightly through the gleaming windows that surround both sides of the corner room. It is so large and spacious. Looking outside, I can see a large weeping willow swaying. The tree is as tall as this three-story school. I imagine myself sitting in the front row of the classroom, concentrating only on myself, my education, and my future.

"That is for sure, Sean. Summer vacation always goes by too fast, doesn't it? I enjoy my summers, but I am also very excited about the new school year and all its challenges. I always look forward to meeting some wonderful new students. It is a pleasure meeting you today, Francie."

"It is so nice meeting you too. I look forward to being in your class," I say, smiling.

"Miss O'Grady, have a great school year," says Sean.

"It was so nice seeing you again. Have a great year too."

As we walk out of her room and into the hallway, I am thinking that I will have to really study her subject, Latin, and it may be difficult. I probably will have to work harder than I thought.

"You know, Sean, I have never taken a language before."

"You will do great, and Latin will help you with a lot of your subjects you will be taking also."

After we find where all my classes will be, I realize there is so much for me to get ready for the start of school. I have to get notebooks, a calendar to keep track of my assignments, and other school supplies I am sure I will need. I have to get my outfits ready also. As we saunter back to the apartment, I am getting a little anxious, and my mind is wandering.

As we get nearer to the spot where the dog was killed this morning, I realize that the boys were really in great danger. We are so fortunate that nothing terrible happened today. I don't know what I would do if something awful did happen.

"Are you getting excited Francie about Tuesday's start of school?"

"Yes, I am. You are always so thoughtful, Sean. Thanks for helping today since it makes it so much easier for me to start school when I have had a walk-through and a class schedule for me to keep."

I give Sean a big hug and a kiss goodbye. I am a little stressed, but I know I just have to do what needs to be done to get my life started. I need to do first things first.

As his long strides take him already halfway down the street, I loudly yell, "I am so looking forward to seeing you Tuesday, Sean!"

"I can't wait, Francie! This will be my best school year yet!" he hollers back, waving.

I race up the stairs and through the door and into the parlor so as not forget one single thought that is now racing through my mind. In my diary, I quickly write, "It's finally here! My future achievements begin right now! I am going to be so dedicated to my studies and what I want to do with my life. I am so glad that Sean will be there with me to help guide me through this new adventure."

Tuesday is finally here, and I am so excited that I get up with the sun. After breakfast, Mary and Austin are getting ready for their first day of school. I see that my brother has come to terms with his classroom assignment. This morning, he even seems to be looking forward to the start of school. Mary is getting her supplies ready and putting them together in her school satchel.

I have been primping all morning because I want to look my best when I meet my new school chums and teachers. I finally decide to wear the outfit I wore to see the Statue of Liberty with Sean. It will bring me luck. Sitting at the kitchen table with Mama, I'm thinking about how I can be successful this school year. Finally, I see Sean through the window, so I finish my coffee quickly. I'm so happy he's here.

"Mama, Sean is outside, waiting for me." I grab my schoolbag. I quickly kiss Mother on her forehead while she is slowly sipping her steaming morning coffee in her blue flannel nightgown. She is so huggable that I have to run back and give her a big embrace. She is my inspiration.

"Good luck, my dear. I hope you have a great first day. Remember what my papa used to say, darling, 'Get good marks!'"

"Thanks, Mama. I certainly will," I respond, and I scurry with my school bag and lunch as I run out the front door.

"Good morning, Francie. You look wonderful this beautiful morning. How are you doing?" asks Sean.

"I'm really nervous! I don't think I slept at all last night, Sean. How are you doing this morning?"

"I'm looking forward to getting the school year started," Sean replies.

It doesn't take us very long to get to Newark High School as I try to keep up with Sean's long steps. I am so glad we can start our day together. Taking a deep breath and a few quick footsteps into the building, I try to smile, but my lips are quivering. There are so many students here; the halls are so crowded that it is intimidating.

Thankfully, Sean escorts me to my first-hour class, which is science with Mr. Kaplan. The morning went by fast, and Sean and I have lunch together, which makes the afternoon even easier. On the way home, I feel relieved and happy; getting the first day completed has really helped my mood. My classes are manageable, and I just have to work hard and keep up with all the assignments.

"Sean, I think my favorite class is science. Mr. Kaplan explained that he is going to teach us about scientific discoveries. His class is going to be really interesting."

"That is exciting, for sure! I think my favorite class is human anatomy, but I will have to work really hard to memorize all the terminology I will need to know for this course," responds Sean.

"I know it will be challenging, but you are so smart, and I know you will do absolutely wonderful! Sean, it's so fun having lunch together."

"I'm looking forward to tomorrow—that's for sure, Francie."

Before we know it, we have completed the first week of school, and we have gotten our everyday formula started. I now have to juggle my chores at home, help Mrs. Ryan, complete homework, and try to have some free time from all the work. Finally, the weekend is here, and I am up early this glorious Saturday morning. I am thankful for some downtime. Looking out the window in the parlor, I see the leaves are now changing from their summer greens to shades of rust and yellow. The stunning maple tree in our front yard has become a splendid shade of scarlet.

The slow shifting of the seasons brings such an assortment of brilliant color to Newark. Fall leaves carry their own earthy scent and vibrant shades. Autumn has got to be my favorite season. Since the nights have become cooler and the days shorter, we know it won't be too long before those lovely leaves will shrivel, drop to the ground, and become part of the earthly landscape, foreshadowing winter's presence.

I grab a cup of hot coffee and head outdoors, where Mary and Austin are playing. As I walk out the front door, I can't help but recall the policeman chasing the rabid dog that was so close to Austin; I try to put that awful thought out of my mind this lovely autumn morning. I survey the area around our apartment, and the coast is clear of any packs of wild dogs. As I sit down on the stoop, the brilliant warm sun is shining on the leaves of the tree, now reflecting into my eyes.

Mary and Austin are kicking a ball around on the lawn. Austin notices a paper bag on the pavement. Inquisitively, of course, he picks up the sack and peeks inside. When he sees what it is, he screams loudly and throws the bag high in the air while its contents fall down into Mary's hair.

"Francie, come quickly!" he yells.

I jump up fast as I can while spilling most of my coffee all over the porch. On Mary's head, there are what appears to be little white worms struggling to escape from where they just landed. Mary is screaming at the top of her voice.

"What in the world are these?" yells Mary as she is now running around the front yard, screaming while making a track of large circles around the yard, and finally slows down standing next to me. How funny that sweet girl is! I try to calm her down so I can remove the little invaders from where they landed in her hair.

"Did these nasty little worms just appear out of nowhere, Francie?" asks Austin.

"They look like worms," I answer as I'm taking them out of her hair one by one, but they are actually the larvae of flies. Flies land on something like food that must have been rotting in the paper bag you picked up, and then the flies laid their eggs inside of the sack. These eggs are called maggots and will grow big and turn into flies. Living things just don't appear magically. A long time ago, people used to think that flies would just appear out of rotting meat, but that is not possible since living things can only come from things that already exist. That old idea was called spontaneous generation. They thought in those days that mice could come out of rotting meat that was left in a barn.

"Yuck!" responds Austin. "Those maggots on the ground smell disgusting, and they look as bad as they smell!"

"Francie, you really learn a lot in school," remarks Mary as she's shaking her head and itching her scalp.

"You will learn that in your classes, too. It was actually Dr. Louis Pasteur who discovered that living things can only come from living things. He put some broth in a container, and when air got into it, all kinds of bacteria grew inside. When no particles got in, it stayed clean and fresh. Bacteria, which are little bugs that can only be seen under a microscope, come from other bacteria. Bacteria can cause diseases and make people sick, and that's why I hate flies, because you never know where they have been."

"Francie, there is so much to know about things. I want to study just like you!"

"You will, Mary! Just be patient!"

I am now back on the porch with another cup of coffee, enjoying the day. I think I am off to a good start with the school year. That reminds me; I have lots of homework to finish this weekend. Oh well!

Chapter 9

It is a beautiful Saturday but a little brisk this October morning; I am walking over to help Mrs. Ryan today. It seems in no time I am already over to their house.

"Oh my gosh!" I scream. What am I seeing? "Heavens, no!" I yell.

As I quickly run up to the chicken coop to collect the eggs, I notice that many of Mrs. Ryan's white Leghorn chickens are lying still and lifeless on the ground. I can't believe she has lost what appears to be half her flock. What is so sad is that some of the little baby chicks are gone, too. As I walk closer, I see a huge dark-brown rat perched on top of the coup. His teeth are extremely sharp; he has a disgusting long thin tail. His little red eyes are glaring. He does not move but continues staring directly at me.

As I get closer to the chicken coup, he suddenly leaps toward me, snarling, never taking his eyes off his prey. Luckily, there next to me is a long shovel leaning on the shed. I grab it quickly and, defending myself, swing it as hard as I can, smashing him dead center. His body goes flying, while his head is stuck on the shovel. How horrid!

At that moment, Mrs. Ryan comes running out of the house. "Francie, are you all right?"

"I am fine, Mrs. Ryan. That vicious rat was coming after me," I explain.

"Oh my goodness! Look what he did to my darling chickens!"

As Mrs. Ryan sees the condition of her flock, she begins to cry, so I need to get her back into the house and try to calm her down. As I wait for Sean to come and help me get the yard ready for winter, I decide to make Mrs. Ryan a cup of black coffee and some breakfast of a poached egg and a piece of dark toast.

"When Sean gets here, he will have some ideas of how to fix the coop so those rats won't come back," I remark.

"That is a great idea, Francie," she replies as she sips her coffee slowly. Her tears have subsided. She grabs a fork and slowly cuts a tiny piece of egg, which she gradually puts in her mouth. She knows she needs nourishment for her and the baby. There is such sadness in her eyes.

Staring out the window, I see Sean finally coming up through the yard. "Mrs. Ryan, I am going outside since Sean is here. Please don't worry about anything. Sean will take care of everything."

As I walk out of the screen door, there is a surprised look on Sean's face.

"I guess I can tell what happened here, Francie."

"I am so thankful that you are here to help, Sean."

"Let us start by burying the poor dead chickens and what is left of the rat," he decides.

"Sean, that nasty animal was coming right at me. Thankfully, the shovel was there so I could protect myself," I add.

"We probably should put some metal doors on the coop and make sure the chicken feed is stored far away from those nasty critters," explains Sean.

"Yea, Francie, those brown rats can be vicious. That reminds me. Do you remember hearing stories about the black rats that carried the bubonic plague throughout Europe during the Middle Ages?"

"How awful," I respond.

"It was actually the fleas the rats carried that brought the disease from the trading ships from all over the world to the harbors of Europe. Many of the sailors on those ships died before they could return home. People had no way of knowing what caused such death and destruction. The disease was called Black Death because the victims had black boils on their skin that oozed blood and pus from their sores. They would die wretchedly in their beds with great pain, vomiting, and high fevers. Many doctors and priests servicing those poor souls would also perish with the sick and the suffering, never to leave those places alive. Nobody then knew what caused the plague. It was so terrifying for those poor, fearful souls who knew that with the coming of warm spring weather and flowers blooming, the death rate would soon climb again."

"Sean, let's imagine that the plague is here. It's the 1200s, and we are in Italy. We have come to bury the dead who have died from the disease."

"No way, Francie! That does not sound like a very fun game to play. Let's just get this done, please."

Once the task of burying those poor creatures is completed, we hurry into the house to check on Mrs. Ryan. Of course, we have to wash our hands over and over thoroughly for a long time, scrubbing with strong washing powder. What a disgusting task to start the day. So far, I have not enjoyed my morning. A cup of coffee seems to calm my nerves.

"How are you doing, Mrs. Ryan?" I ask.

"I am okay, I guess," she responds.

"Mrs. Ryan, I will come by first thing in the morning to put some metal doors on the chicken coop. Also, I moved the chicken feed into the screened-in porch, placing it in a sealed metal drum that was in the yard," explains Sean. "That will keep them away."

"Thanks for your help, my dears. I am doing better now, but I think I am going to stay indoors. When Danny takes his nap, I will lie down. If you could, please clean up what is left of the garden. Any green tomatoes out there can be wrapped with newspaper and put down in the cellar. They will soon ripen by themselves, and we can eat fresh tomatoes for quite a while. Please cut down the remains of the flowers and trim the lilac bushes so they will be ready to bloom next spring. I appreciate all your help," she continues. "Francie, as always, I am very thankful for your kindness."

Sean and I start our chores. He feels the lawn should be mowed one more time before the snow falls, so he is cutting the long grass also. The wind is picking up now, and there is a chill in the air. I quickly grab what seems to be fifty green tomatoes off their vines. I place them carefully inside a paper sack, and I run down to the cellar to wrap each one in newspaper and place them on the old table under the window. Those tomatoes will be a delicious addition to some great salads.

Presently, I am trimming those big lilac bushes, which will be flowering again come May. Next, I cut down the rest of the perennials in the garden so they, too, will come back to blossom in the spring. The gold black-eyed Susans have wilted and will need a fresh start for next summer, so I am cutting them back also. They are a hearty plant and do very well here in Newark with all our types of weather. I love those pretty flowers, and they blossom all summer and fall. Soon, Sean is done with the yard, and he places the mower back in the shed.

"You know, Sean, I believe there is nothing we can't do if life forces us to accomplish something. We just have to do what may seem the impossible with the daring we will need at that particular moment in time."

"I agree, Francie. We never know what hand life is going to deal us, but we need to face it at that time with all the resolution and strength that is necessary to finish the task," Sean adds. "You didn't know this morning what the day would bring, and you handle everything with such daring and courage, Francie."

"Yes, and I am really brave when you are here helping me, that's for sure," I add. "Look how dark it is getting already, Sean. The days are becoming so much shorter."

"I'm so glad we were able to finish the chores for Mrs. Ryan," responds Sean. "The weather is definitely changing. We better say goodbye and get you home before your mother starts worrying about you."

"Yes, Sean, I promised Mother that I will get up early for church tomorrow, so we better get going," I add.

After telling Mrs. Ryan goodbye, Sean walks me home to the front steps. I give him a big hug and a kiss. I really don't want him to leave so soon.

I am thinking, *What would I ever do without him?*

"Thank you so much for your help today," I reply. "I can always depend on you, Sean."

"It was so nice spending the afternoon with you, Francie. Thank you for the pleasure of your company," he exclaims with a big smile.

I feel so pleased that we could be there for Mrs. Ryan today. Sean is really such a nice guy. He is always smiling and happy to help and positive about everything. I am so lucky to have him in my life. All of today's accomplishments are going through my mind as I get ready for bed. I am so exhausted that I fall right asleep.

The weekend is going by fast as it always does. Before we know it, it's Sunday morning, and the Fitzgeralds are getting ready for Mass as we promised Mother we would all go to church today as a family. As Mary and I are getting ready, I notice that she does not seem to be herself. There is sadness in her eyes, and lately, she never seems to smile much.

"Francie, I am not looking forward to going to school tomorrow," Mary said sadly.

"You always love school, Mary. What is going on with you?"

"Well," she begins to explain. "There is this new girl in our class that has been here for about a month. Her name is Beatrice, and even though I try to get along with her, she is always picking on me constantly every chance she gets. The other day on the playground, she kicked me with her short, pudgy leg, and I went flying in the dirt during recess. She laughed out loud in front of the other kids. I was so embarrassed. My knee was really bleeding, and there was so much gravel in my cut that I had to go to the nurse's office to get it cleaned up and bandaged."

"I can't believe she did that to you, Mary!"

"The other day, I heard her talking about me before class began. She makes fun of the lunch I bring to school. She belittles anything I say when I am talking to the other kids at recess. When she's captain, she never picks me for her team. Francie, she's making me miserable."

"Have you told Mother so she can talk to your teacher about it?" I ask.

"I don't want to cause any trouble. I thought it would be better to just ignore her, and maybe she would stop," answers Mary.

"If that's not working, you need to tell the teacher or have Mother explain what is going on. You can't allow Beatrice to have such power over you, Mary," I explain. "She does not respect you, and you must demand respect from her. Beatrice is a bully!"

"You're right, Francie. I've let it go way too long," she explains. "First thing Monday morning, I will tell sister what's going on. If it doesn't improve, I will tell Mother."

"Let me know what happens. You always enjoy school. That girl should not have any influence over you at all," I remind Mary.

I notice how lovely the morning is while sitting at the kitchen table looking out the window as I slowly pour myself a cup of coffee from that old pot that used to be grandma's. Today I am wearing my new blue and white checkered skirt and a blue sweater Mother knitted for me. The family is all dressed for church as we begin our walk to nine o'clock Mass together.

Our father looks so handsome in his blue suit, carrying little Colin in his arms. Mother is wearing her new green dress, which makes her eyes sparkle. Even Austin looks spiffy with his blue pants and new sweater. It is a cool morning, and I notice as we are walking that there is a heavy scent of burning leaves that always permeates the neighborhood this time of the year. It is a smell that immediately brings me back to childhood memories of raking leaves and building bonfires.

Today, Father Early is saying Mass. I think he is the greatest! His sermons are short and to the point, and he never rambles; he is so young and so personable. After the service, we all go downstairs for coffee and doughnuts, which is great since I am completely starving.

"Come on, Mary, let's get in line, and we can bring everyone their breakfast," I explain.

"Okay, Francie," Mary replies in her usual agreeable tone.

All of a sudden, as we are walking up to the counter in the back of the hall, Mary stops in her tracks and refuses to budge another step. Her mood has become very somber. She is glaring at a short, heavy girl marching toward us, carrying a tray filled with cups of coffee, glazed doughnuts, and a few glasses of milk.

"Mary, what's wrong?" I ask in a low voice.

"Francie, that is the girl I was telling you about, that is Beatrice walking toward us with the tray."

"Oh, really!" I reply in a sarcastic tone.

As Beatrice turns right next to me, I immediately, without even thinking about it, stick out my foot in front of her, tripping her forward to the floor. The brown tray goes flying up in the air and crashes deafeningly on the tile. Beatrice falls down hard on her knees! There are doughnuts, milk, and coffee in a sickening mixture all over the checkered tile floor. Beatrice slowly rises and grabs her knee with a grimace of pain upon her red face. She is now looking at me, and I, of course, say nothing but give her a huge smile and a glare.

While we are getting our breakfast, Mary is laughing hysterically. "Nice move, girl," she says. "You know, Francie, I am really looking forward to school Monday. Thanks!"

I feel bad doing that in the church basement, but Beatrice really has it coming. I would never let anyone be so mean to my little sister. That's a Sunday we won't soon forget, and neither will Beatrice. Hopefully, things will improve at school, and the girl has learned her lesson.

That evening, we eat a roasted chicken dinner with browned potatoes and carrots and rutabagas. We only get chicken dinner once in a while on Sundays because it is rather pricey right now. I eat my chicken leg very slowly, savoring every bite as I chuckle to myself about what happened this morning. I make sure not to mention the prank, not wanting to upset Mother. Rutabaga is a vegetable I am not too crazy about, but I know it is good for us to eat, so I force myself to finish that big yellow root.

Mother's famous cabbage salad is out of this world. Aunt Molly made the most delicious chocolate cake. All in all, it's a great Sunday with all of us spending the day together. My homework is finally done, and I am exhausted and ready for bed. I am having a little trouble getting to sleep, which I sometimes do on Sunday nights.

Monday morning is here already. Thunder crash, and several bright strikes of lightning light up the bedroom, making it very difficult for me to get out of my warm bed. The howling wind rattling the window doesn't help either, but I manage with all my strength. The walk to school is not pleasant, either. Sean and I are under one umbrella we share, but it is doing little to protect us from the sideways downpour. As we rush into school and away from the rain, my feet are soaked, and I am shivering. I am glad I have Mr. Kaplan for the first period since his class, at least, is the most interesting of the day.

"Have a good morning, Francie," Sean remarks. "I will see you in the lunchroom." Sean smiles as he hurries upstairs to his anatomy class.

"You too," I remark. "See you soon, Sean."

Before I go to class, I scamper quickly into the girls' room to dump the cold rainwater out of my soggy shoes and into the sink. Then I take my dripping stockings off and put them inside a sack in the corner of my schoolbag. I'm now putting a comb through my drenched hair and placing it swiftly into a ponytail to try to look at least halfway decent for the first-hour class. Next, I try to compose myself as I run into Mr. Kaplan's room before I am late for class. I always like to look nice for Mr. Kaplan.

Getting out my notebook and pencil, I take my seat, which is the first desk in the first row, where I can easily see the board and see my teacher, too.

"Hi, Anna."

"Hi, Francie. Can you believe the storm we had this morning?"

"The thunder woke me so early, but I really didn't want to get up and go out in this weather," I respond.

Just then, Mr. Kaplan walks into class with a newspaper in hand.

"Good morning, class." Mr. Kaplan always greets us with a smile as if he is so glad to be sharing his knowledge. He makes learning so fun and interesting; his class is never boring.

"Class," our teacher begins as he is staring out the window past the rain to a different place and time. "I have a copy from yesterday's newspaper, the *New York World*." Mr. Kaplan begins reading slowly in a loud voice the headline of the article: "A Fourteen-Year-Old Youth Saves Children in Jura, France."

Of course, this headline grabs my attention. Looking around the class, I can see my fellow classmates are in awe as much as I.

He continues reading, "Jean-Baptiste Jupille, a shepherd boy in the meadows of France, saved six other boys who were taking care of a herd of cattle when a vicious, rabid dog chased after them. Jupille threw himself on the canine, allowing the other children to escape. While being bitten several times on his right hand, he ended up muzzling the dog with his whip to free its clenching grip. The dog then locked the boy's hand in its powerful jaws. Finally, Jean-Baptiste took off his shoe and smashed the animal in its head, killing him instantly."

Mr. Kaplan continues the session by explaining what happens next. "It was decided that Jupille needed to travel to Paris, France, to see Dr. Louis Pasteur, who had a serum that could be injected in the boy to save him from contracting rabies. The boy endured daily shots of the vaccine for several days to clear the germ from his system. Later, he was released and went home cured by Dr. Pasteur. What is scary about rabies, class, is that it is a disease that attacks the central nervous system, and most victims do not survive their ordeal."

This is yet another victim of a rabid animal. This young hero from the French countryside was saved by the rabies vaccine. I am here sitting almost in a daze. I feel the pain of that poor boy. My eyes are tearing up. I have seen the snarling teeth, the vengeful eyes, the foaming jaws when the boys were so close to that rabid dog the other day. Having been bitten so many times, it is hard to believe Jupille could even survive such an attack. Here is yet another accomplishment of Pasteur to tell Sean.

Now thoughts of Jupille, Joseph Meister, and the dead fox by the lake are all going so rapidly through my mind at the same time, making me so dizzy that I have to close my eyes. Suddenly, I feel such a cold chill going up and down my spine that I shiver once again. Looking up at Mr. Kaplan, I desperately try to escape my fears.

Our instructor is now explaining how the rabies serum is made and how injections have to be given in a certain way for several days. This vaccine will fight the germ of rabies, and Jean-Baptiste Jupille has survived his torment. Mr. Kaplan also clarifies how Dr. Pasteur discovered this cure through his research about germs and the diseases they can cause. Since the microscope is a tool scientists use to study little one-cell microbes, our teacher is now passing out an assignment on this instrument; we need to complete it using the diagram in our textbooks.

Presently, I cannot concentrate on doing anything right now. Mr. Kaplan has no clue about all the apprehensions that have been racing through my thoughts. For several minutes, I sit still, staring out the window, and for a long time, I do absolutely nothing.

Chapter 10

I t is the first of December, and we cannot believe how mild the weather has been these last few days. Every inch of snow has completely disappeared from our last blizzard; it's so much fun to walk to school this morning with the warm wind blowing in our faces.

On the way home, Sean and I decide to walk the long way, which we have not done for quite awhile, enjoying the mild day. Last month, we had the worst snowstorm I can ever remember. There was terrible flooding on our beautiful Jersey shore, making me long for our carefree days of summer. Everyone calls it a nor'easter, which is when warm air from the gulf meets the cold air from up north.

The air was so unbelievably frigid. We could even see these huge breaking waves coming from the sea so far onto the land. That windy storm brought fifteen inches of snow to Newark in one day. We tried to dress as warm as we could, so we added layers of sweaters and heavy socks. The warm mittens Mother made for us came in handy. The only good thing about the storm was that we got to miss school for a few days. I just loved sleeping in the morning under a warm quilt.

Today's warm weather has given me newfound energy. Immediately, when I get home, I finish all my science homework. Next, I mind Collin while Mother starts the oxtail vegetable beef soup, browning big chunks of meat slowly on the stove. As I put Collin in his high chair, I decide to help Mother with supper. Looking in the icebox, I grab celery, carrots, and onions and then start cutting the vegetables up in small pieces. Then Mama hands me the potatoes from the cupboard, which I quickly peel and dice.

We combine all the ingredients into Grandma's iron pot. Mother is now cutting up ripe tomatoes in quarters to throw in for added flavor. She is also adding salt, pepper, and parsley to the mixture. The succulent aroma passes through the apartment. I am ready for supper right this moment!

By this time, Mary and Austin have made their way home from school.

"Francie, can you believe how warm it was today?" asks Mary.

"I know," I respond with a huge smile. "Isn't it just marvelous?"

"Francie, does that mean that we will get an early spring?" asks Austin.

"Oh, I really don't know for sure, Austin, but I really do hope so," I respond. "Mother, did you see that big full moon last night? It was quite strange and looked as though it were really made of cheese. It was unusually large—the biggest moon I have ever seen."

"Yes, honey, it was lovely. The color was quite rare, wasn't it?"

"The bright light reflecting from the moon outside my bedroom window startled me from a deep sleep in the middle of the night. After I woke up, it took forever before I could go back to sleep, and when I finally did doze, I had a very peculiar dream. I was on this huge ship out in the ocean, and there were all these enormous waves throwing us about, making me so very sick. It was so unbelievably cold too, and I couldn't seem to warm up. In my dream, I could see the big waves while I was lying on my cot. Looking out the porthole, I could see the same large, orange full moon that was shining in my bedroom before I went to bed. Also, it was so strange that in my dream, there was the sound of constant weeping in the distance. That dream was so unusual because I couldn't tell where the crying was coming from. When I got out of bed this morning, I felt so dizzy and had such an eerie feeling of not really knowing if I was on sea or land."

"That is really odd, Francie. Sometimes we dream outlandish things, dear, not really knowing what they mean," explains Mother as she stirs the soup and adds more pepper. "You are safe and sound, my girl, here with your family."

"I just am not sure what it means. It was so real!"

"Mother," interrupts Mary, "I forgot to tell you that we have started working on our play today, and we will have practice after school next week every day except Friday."

"Oh, I am so glad, honey, since I know you have been looking forward to the playacting. It sounds like lots of fun," chimes in Mother.

We hear the squeaking of the back door opening slowly, and there in the kitchen now in front of us is our father, who never gets home from work this early! He is carrying a big paper sack in his arms. We all run up to greet him. He gives Mother a kiss hello and hands her a box of chocolates with the word *Cordials* on the front of it in big red letters. Of course, we all start to laugh. Also, in the bag are several large oranges and some black licorice sticks.

"Dear, you are home so early today," replies Mother.

"I picked a fine day not to work the second shift," explains Daddy.

"How are you today?" I ask him.

"This weather has put me in a great mood, my girl. How was school, Francie?"

"I had such a great day and got a B on that difficult book report I turned in on Monday."

"That's great, my dear! Keep getting those good grades."

It is a wonderful afternoon! The weather is so exceptional, the soup is ready to enjoy, and the Fitzgeralds are eating supper all together tonight.

"What's new with you, Austin?" asks Daddy.

"We got to go outdoors for recess today! It was so much fun running around the schoolyard and playing ball. In fact, they gave us extra free time since the weather was so nice."

"Daddy, I got a part in the school play," chimes in Mary. "I play one of the children in *A Christmas Carol*. We will perform before Christmas vacation starts. You have to come see us! Promise?" she adds.

"I am so proud of you, Mary. I surely will," responds Daddy.

The Fitzgerald family sits down for a delightful supper of beef soup and warm soda bread fresh from the oven and dotted with lots of chewy raisins. The oranges we eat for dessert are so sweet we feel like we're eating fruit just picked from their branches.

Mother opens her box of chocolates and gives each of us a sample, and they are the best ever, filled with big juicy cherries. We each also get some licorice sticks. After, Austin and Mary help clear the dishes off the kitchen table, while I begin washing Grandma's beautiful white, porcelain soup bowls carefully.

"Austin, why don't you get to your arithmetic homework?" advises Mother.

"Bring your book here to the table, son, and let me help you get started," suggests Daddy.

While Mary is drying the dishes, I have a hilarious thought. "Mary, how is Beatrice doing?" I start to chuckle, and she starts laughing out loud, remembering that morning in the church basement the day I got back at Beatrice.

"She has been a lot nicer to me since that day after church. She never picks on me anymore, and I thank you for that. I try to just get along with her. I don't think we'll ever be best friends. I'm going to start reading Dickens's *Christmas Carol* tonight and start preparing for my part in the play, Francie. I am so excited. I really can't wait. It's going to be so much fun."

"I will be in the parlor in a few minutes with you, Mary, as I need to do some reading tonight, too."

I get out my diary to write down what happened in my crazy vision from last night. When I finish making entries, I feel so cold and dizzy, like I was still on the ship in my dream. That is really strange. I am having a hard time concentrating on my book I need to read for English. I look at the clock, and I can't believe it is eleven already. Mary has gone to bed, and so has everyone else. I do feel drowsy, so I should go right to sleep.

As I walk into my bedroom, I see that huge cream-colored moon outside my window, lighting up the night sky. This is the exact same moon I saw last night when I was sleeping. It was hanging over the bow of the ship. Lying in bed, I now feel as cold as I felt last night when I dreamed I was out at sea. In an attempt to warm up, I force myself out of bed and put on my heavy white socks since my feet are as cold as the frozen icicles that hang from the roof during a winter storm.

On the chair in the corner is my blue, wool blanket. When I look toward the window, I grab the cover and jump quickly back in bed. As I lie here quivering, staring up at the moon, an unnerving feeling comes over me, and I am so frightened that it is forever before I finally fall asleep.

When I awake, sunshine has replaced the light of the moon. But now my mind is in a thick fog, like I did not get any rest.

What time is it? I wonder. *Am I late for school?*

I suddenly remember that today is teachers' meetings, so there is no school for students. Forcing myself out from under all those blankets, I feel so lazy walking to the kitchen. Pouring a big cup of coffee should help.

Why am I not in a better mood? I wonder.

"Good morning, my darlin'. How are you?" asks Mother.

"I am a little tired. I guess I slept late."

"I have some oatmeal on the stove for you, Francie. Austin and Mary are already outdoors since it is such a fine day."

"Thanks," I reply as I silently and slowly try to eat, leaving most of it in the bowl.

"Mother, I think I will go outdoors and get some fresh air."

Sitting on the porch, I am fearful again, just like last night. My body begins to shiver even though the sun is shining warmly in my face. Feeling so anxious, I decide to go for a walk to try to calm my nerves. *What is going on with me? Why am I so afraid?* I am now walking very fast in the direction of Mrs. Ryan's house.

The fresh air does seem to help a little, and my apprehension gives me energy. Walking several blocks, I see up ahead Austin, little Eddie, and Paddy Reynolds, his chum. I also see Willie Lane, who is an older boy who works as a messenger in the neighborhood. They seem to be having a great time laughing and talking. Mary is on the porch swing with Mrs. Ryan and little Danny.

"Hey, Austin, isn't it a great day? Maybe we will have an early spring after all."

At that precise moment, I have an awful feeling of something evil approaching. Turning my head quickly, I see that there are now four dogs galloping down Mrs. Ryan's street like an invading army. They are so close I can hear them panting. I let out an awful scream but not in time.

The large shaggy dog in the lead is dripping foam out of his mouth, growling ferociously while staring at Austin. Suddenly it leaps on Austin, and the poor boy lets out a most terrifying shriek. The wicked mongrel takes a mouthful out of his arm.

"Oh, my God! No!" I scream as I run to him.

As I try to comfort my brother, the dog leaps on Paddy next and, without hesitating, pushes him on the ground and chomps on his hand. Not having had enough, the mongrel then jumps on Willie, who now has a bite on his forehead, which is bleeding profusely. Next, the cur focuses his madness on little Eddie, who is screaming while attempting to run backward, away from those vicious, staring eyes, but the boy does not have the strength. He falls backward, hitting his head on the ground, while the dog takes a bite out of his leg.

The victims are now crying all in unison. Mrs. Ryan quickly places Danny in his carriage pushing him as she runs down to her son Eddie as fast as she can, falling down almost in a faint to the sidewalk. I am concerned about Mrs. Ryan and the little one she's carrying. Mary is screaming as she races down the lawn to comfort Austin and wraps her arms around his shoulders.

Everything has happened so quickly. By now, the dogs have taken off to find other victims. I am just sitting on the street, shaking, not knowing what to do. The dreaded monster I have feared for so long has done its evil deeds. I must do something. I must be brave. I must have courage. I get up and walk slowly to Mrs. Ryan, who is sitting on the ground, holding Eddie in her arms, trying to comfort the boy.

"Mrs. Ryan, are you okay?"

"I'm all right, Francie."

"Mary, go get Mother and have her meet us at Dr. O'Gorman's office."

"Come on, Mrs. Ryan, we have to get these boys to the doctor," I softly request as I help her up.

Mrs. Ryan pushes the carriage with little Danny and has Eddie walk, leaning on the buggy, as she slowly takes small steps down the street. I pick up Austin and let him rest on my shoulder as we walk quietly together. The other boys are inching painstakingly, but before we know it, we are finally here.

Dr. O'Gorman comes out to help. His shoulders are hunched, and his face looks so sad. He grabs Eddie and comes back for Austin. His face is flushed, and his hands are shaking as he lifts

Austin onto the table. The doctor is visibly moved. He looks so different, and he has aged so much. His blue eyes are sagging, and he's not standing up straight. The rest of the boys walk in on their own accord.

"Francie, I am going to cauterize their wounds," remarks the doctor, who seems to be almost in a daze.

"Doctor, if they do have rabies, burning their wounds with a hot iron will not help. It will only give them a big scar and not save them from the rabies infection. The boys need the vaccine. Don't you remember how Dr. Pasteur was able to inoculate those children and save them from the terrible disease?"

"Why, yes, you are right, Francie. I don't know what I am thinking. Help me clean their wounds. Mrs. Ryan, could you please get the bandages out of the cupboard and help dress their injuries?" the doctor asks.

"You know it is just a matter of time before it will be too late for these boys, and nothing will help them. That dog was foaming at the mouth. He definitely has rabies. The boys need to get the vaccine as soon as possible. That is the only cure."

"Yes, Francie, I will cable Dr. Pasteur. He has to see them as soon as possible."

Mrs. Ryan and I assist the doctor in washing their injuries and helping to bandage their wounds. My darling brother seems to have gotten the worst of it. His elbow was bitten so badly through his jacket that the bone is showing and blood is oozing from his arm. Lying here now, he looks so frail and thin. My tears are coming down so fast that I can hardly see him lying in front of me. He is in such pain that he can't stop moaning.

"Francie, there was spray coming out of the dog's mouth while he was tearing into my arm, and his eyes had such evil in them," Austin cries.

"Yes, honey, I know." I try to be calm as I remember that close call the boys had in the front yard when three dogs ran by our house. Also, I recall the Fourth of July picnic when Aunt Molly's blue-ribbon pie was knocked over by wild dogs.

I am wondering if it was the same dog that attacked the boys today since he looked so familiar. Abruptly, I feel the nausea returning. I run to the sink to throw up. I have to sit down since my head is spinning. Now, I hear Mother and Mary walking through the door.

"Oh no!" screams Mother. She falls on Austin and wraps her arms around him and kisses him over and over again.

"Oh my goodness, Francie! What are we going to do?"

"Dr. O'Gorman is going to cable Dr. Pasteur in Paris. He will know what to do."

"But, Francie, it is so far and will take so long for them to get to France," Mother explains.

"It will be fine, Mother. Don't worry. We will figure it out."

As I am bandaging Austin's bloody arm, I see the ugly, dead fox sitting in its own blood down by the lake, a vision that never completely leaves my mind. I can't believe what has happened today. As I sit on a stool beside my brother, I put my throbbing head into my hands, close my eyes, and pray reverently that God will be with them and the boys will be saved.

Chapter 11

D r. O'Gormon has sent a cable to Paris, explaining the attack on the boys, and Dr. Louis Pasteur has responded, "If you think the boys are in danger, send the children immediately." (Hansen, 2009)

"Francie, we need to act quickly to get the kids to France, but how? It will be so very expensive," Dr. O'Gorman explains.

"There is a way we can do it, Doctor. Do you remember how the money was raised for the pedestal for the Statue of Liberty? Joseph Pulitzer invited his readers to donate funds, and each of these contributors had their names and donations printed in the *New York World*. They collected over $100,000 worth of contributions mostly from small gifts. Why don't you write the newspaper a letter explaining what happened? I am sure that it will help encourage people to donate."

"What a great idea, Francie! I forgot all that, my girl. Isn't that funny that I didn't remember about Pulitzer printing all those names? Sometimes, I think I'm losing my memory. You are quite cool under pressure, girl, and I appreciate all your help. Do you think you could help me write the letter, Francie?"

"I would love to help you, Doctor," I responded.

It didn't take us long to compose the letter, and it was printed the very next day after we submitted it to the newspaper. The article explained who the boys are and how they've been attacked by a vicious dog in Newark, New Jersey. The article also said that the boys most likely have rabies and that this is a disease that can be treated now after the individuals have been bitten. We let everyone know that the victims will need to have enough funds to take a ship from New York to France in order for them to get the lifesaving treatment from Dr. Pasteur in Paris. Also, it is necessary for the kids to have enough warm clothing for their journey crossing the ocean in the winter. They will need a hospital room on the ship so they can be cared for while on the trip .

Within a few days, the generous donations are now pouring into the *New York World*. We are so thankful to Mr. Pulitzer and his newspaper and also those caring individuals that give whatever they can for our cause. We see so many of our friends' names in print donating as well; Dr. O'Gorman alone gave fifty dollars. With all the wonderful gifts of money, the boys will be able to get passage across the Atlantic to France, and thankfully, they will receive Dr. Pasteur's assistance.

As usual, people are being so kind and generous, giving what they can. Thankfully, they are also providing that much-needed hospital room for the boys on the ship as well. Even a Newark haberdasher by the name of Sven Hansen is donating sweaters, coats, heavy shoes, and other clothing the boys will need to keep warm on the ocean voyage. All the apparel will be dropped off at Dr. O'Gormon's office.

Austin has been resting comfortably in his bed at home as the good doctor has given him something to help him sleep. On the other hand, I have not been able to sleep very much at all since this terrible attack has happened.

It is five o'clock in the morning, and I might as well get up and start my day and have a cup of coffee. As I walk into the kitchen, I see Mother sitting at the kitchen table as the coffee pot is brewing. It smells so agreeable. It is just what I need.

"Francie, you can't sleep either?"

"No, Mama, I certainly cannot. I've been up for a long while now. Things are going well, but I am still very much worried about my little brother."

"Yes, dear, sleep is not the order of the day. But I am so happy about the donations, Francie. They are certainly a godsend and an answer to our prayers."

"Definitely, it is such a blessing, but, Mother, I'm concerned about Austin since he is a little guy going on a big ship so very far away from home. Remember my dream from the other evening? I heard sobbing and moaning by someone on a large vessel in the middle of the night while we were at sea."

"I am worried about him, too," says Mother as she pours each of us a big cup of hot coffee, adding the usual amount of cream to mine.

For a long while, we sit silently, sipping the hot brew, watching the sun peeking out of the gray clouds. The sunrise has a pink and orange hue now covering the clearing sky. Mother gets the last piece of coffee cake off the counter. It is filled with raisins and nuts, and it is covered with a thick white icing that is so inviting. She cuts it in half, giving one part to each of us and then pours some more coffee.

While I am enjoying the last morsel of this delicious treat, there is a knock on the door. Mama immediately rises to open the side door; it is Dr. O'Gormon. He is wearing a blue coat and a matching checkered blue and white hat, which he removes as he steps into our kitchen.

"Come in, Doctor. Please sit down. Here, sir," she says as she pours him a cup of coffee.

"Thank you, Mrs. Fitzgerald." He takes a big gulp from the large brown cup. "This really hits the spot this chilly morning."

"Well, it is all arranged, ladies," he says as he begins reading word for word from a white sheet of paper. "There is a French Steamer, the *Canada*, that will pick up the children in New York Harbor and take them to Le Havre in the north of France. The ship does have a hospital room, where the boys will be attended by a nurse who will be on board both going there and returning home. Once they arrive in Le Havre, they will then get on a train to Paris, where they will meet Dr. Pasteur that same afternoon. The whole trip will take almost three weeks before they arrive home. They will leave New York on December 9."

I have an idea that I keep thinking about, and I'm getting very anxious since I keep turning it over and over in my mind. Should I mention it now when Father is not here? Will Mother agree? I have to just come out and say it.

"It seems like everything is ready to go," replies Mother.

"Mama, I have a suggestion I would like to share with you and Dr. O'Gormon. Would it be at all possible for me to go with Austin to Paris? I know he will be terrified to go without one of his family members along, and I can help take care of him and make sure he is doing all right. He is so little and helpless. I promise,

Mama, I won't get in the way. I don't want that awful part of my dream of someone sobbing on a ship to be my brother."

"I think that is a wonderful idea, Francie! It sure will take a load off my mind, knowing you will be there with him since he will be gone for such a long time. You are very thoughtful and considerate, my girl. I'm sure your dad will also agree that this is a great plan as he has been awfully worried, too."

"Francie, I think that is a great consideration on your part," replies Dr. O'Gormon. "I need to be going now, ladies, and God be with you and your brother, Francie."

"Thank you for all your help, Doctor," says Mother.

While Doctor O'Gormon goes through the doorway, we see Mrs. Ryan outside on the porch. The doctor lets her in, away from the cold; when he goes, the fierce wind slams the side door shut.

"Good morning, Meg. I could not sleep, and I had so much energy when I got up so early this morning that I decided to walk all the way here. The cold air was quite refreshing."

"Good morning, Katie. Here's a cup of coffee to warm you up, dear."

"Thank you kindly. Well, I will get to the point. I've decided to go along with Eddie on the ship, and since Danny is too young to be left at home with my John working all the time, he will go with us too."

"I think that is so great! Our Francie is going with my Austin!"

"Well, Mrs. Ryan, here is another experience for us," I remark. "I am so glad you will be there, too. I would like to help you and little Danny anyway I can!"

"I feel so relieved that we will be together on this new adventure, Francie. I know I can always depend on you!" she says, smiling.

We all begin to laugh, knowing that we will have another great experience on the ship across the Atlantic. I am so pleased I can go. I feel like I am doing something so important, more important than anything I have ever done before in my life, even more important than my studies.

"I best be getting back home now as John needs to leave for work soon. I must get all our stuff together for the voyage. I will be seeing you soon, Francie."

As Mrs. Ryan leaves, I also feel the need to get everything ready for the trip. I will get my heavy sweaters and other winter clothes sorted. I should pack for Austin too. I am so happy they are giving him warm winter clothes since it will be so frigid on the North Atlantic this time of the year. While sipping the rest of my coffee, I suddenly realize I will have to tell Sean today that I will be going along with Austin on the trip to Europe. That certainly will not be so easy and something I'm not looking forward to doing.

Chapter 12

Sean is outside, waiting to walk me to school like he does every morning, but today will not be quite like any other day. How will I tell him that we will be leaving soon to take a ship far away to France? I will just have to calmly let him know of our plans.

"Good morning, Sean."

"Good morning, Francie. How are you doing? Were you able to sleep last night?"

"I didn't sleep much at all."

As we start walking through the cold wind hitting our faces, the weather has changed again, and the sky looks gray while the heavy clouds look as though they are carrying lots of snow.

I begin slowly by saying, "I don't know how to tell you, my dear. It is very difficult for me to say these words to you, but I must let you know what's on my mind. I have decided to go with Austin on the ship to France since he is too weak and frail to go by himself without a member of his family going along. Mrs. Ryan will accompany Eddie because he is so young, too. She is taking Danny along because there is no one to watch him during the day when his dad is working. It is not going to be easy for her to go, taking both boys, in her condition, and I am glad I will be there to help her, too."

Sean does not say a word, while his facial expression is speaking volumes. His face looks so sad, but I am not saying another word until he does. After a long wait, he finally expresses out loud the thoughts he has been keeping from me as we file slowly to school.

"I understand completely, Francie. I was just kind of surprised by you leaving, that's all. Can I help you in any way? I will get all the school work that you miss and do whatever I can do to make it easier."

"That will be so wonderful, Sean. I appreciate all your kindness. I am going to stop by the office later to explain that I will be leaving soon. Mother has written an excuse letter for my absences for me to give to the principal."

We continue walking, but I can see that Sean's mood has become very subdued. As we get to the school's front steps and all the students are milling, waiting for the bell, Sean grabs my hands and looks directly into my eyes.

"I know you are doing the right thing, Francie. I only wish that I could go with you and watch over you. You know I will miss you so much."

"I will miss you too Sean. It is only for a few weeks, and time always goes by quickly," I explain.

After a little while, he continues, "I was impressed by all the many contributions listed in the *New York World* for the boys' trip to Europe. Last July, when we were going to see the Statue of Liberty, I never dreamed that there would be another fundraiser for kids that had been ravaged by a rabid dog in Newark. When Joseph Meister was bitten six months ago on the Fourth of July, I never thought that Austin and the other boys would get attacked in our very own neighborhood."

"And, Sean, I never imagined that I would be going on a steamer all the way to France with my little brother because he had been bitten by a diseased animal. Remember that time not that long ago when we spoke about having to do things that we need to do with the courage we will need at that moment? I guess this is one of those moments, Sean, and hopefully, I will be able to meet those responsibilities."

The loud ringing of the bell brings me back to the present; most of the students have already filed into the school. Suddenly, Sean grabs me and hugs me ever so tightly. As I look into his big brown eyes, I see tears forming, and I, too, begin to cry as we embrace before we force ourselves to plod slowly into the school. As we walk to our first-hour classes, somehow I know my life will never be the same again. I try to dry my eyes quickly as I go into

Mr. Kaplan's class. I get into my seat and scrunch down, hoping no one will see the tears I'm trying to wipe away. This school day will be one of the longest and most difficult I have ever had to endure!

In every class, especially this last one, my English class, I have been studying the clock, which has moved so slowly as if time were stationary today. Finally, the dismissal bell rings, and as I quickly walk out of the room, there is Sean waiting to walk me home. He greets me with an encouraging smile, and I appreciate him so much more. I try to make these final moments we have together last as I take small steps on the way home while holding his arm so close to me.

"Before you know it, Francie, you will be coming home. I am going to ask Mr. O'Malley to give me added hours at the store while you are gone. Working more will help make the time go much faster. I need to make extra money for school anyway."

"That is so sweet, Sean! I know I will be busy too, and before long, I will be on the voyage home."

"Francie, we should plan a welcome home dinner at Arturo's when you return. We can have some wonderful spaghetti ."

"That's a great idea, Sean. It is such a romantic place, with the large dripping candles on top of the checkered red and white tablecloths. I especially love the singing waiters all dressed up in their fancy black tuxedos."

"That's a date, Francie! I can smell the spicy sauce and the warm, freshly baked bread now."

My mind was so intently thinking about our planned rendezvous that I don't even notice we are right in front of my apartment. Sean puts his arms around me and, with a sweet smile, gives me a tender kiss.

Looking at him now, I'm making sure I won't forget his handsome face, beautiful smile, and kind soul; then I kiss and hug him goodbye.

"Farewell, my dearest Sean. Take care of yourself," I quickly say. I walk up the steps as my eyes begin to water.

"Goodbye, Francie!" I hear him say as he leaves.

Tears are streaming down my cheeks so much now that I can barely see climbing up the steps, never having the courage to look back at Sean. I force myself through the front door and go straight into the parlor and put my head down in my hands, sobbing uncontrollably, trying to take gasps of air. I am now feeling such anxiety and fear all mixed together.

Grabbing my diary out of the drawer, my hand is shaking as I try to write the thoughts I am feeling at this moment. I will miss Sean so much, and I am so very afraid of what the future may bring for all of us. I pray God takes care of Austin and the other boys, too, and that I will have the courage I will need for such a trip across the sea.

There is a heavy weight of responsibility I carry on my shoulders. I have to take each day as it comes and try to do the right thing. The cry has released my anguish and allowed me to finish expressing my thoughts in my dear diary, which will be with me every step of the way on our voyage. Now I need to get Grandma's old valise out of Mother's closet and start packing. The dusty brown case is tattered, ripped on one side, and smells so musty, but it's the only one we have. It will have to do. It will help to clean out the inside with some strong vinegar.

I begin packing my two heavy woolen sweaters and my two long skirts and a long jacket from Mother that I can wear under my heavy coat. I am also getting Austin's warm clothing ready as we are sharing the same suitcase. I will have to thank Mr. Hansen for his kind generosity to my little brother. His clothes are so stylish and will keep him comfortable on the ship.

Time is moving quickly. Tomorrow we will take the ferry to New York, and then on the next day, we will board the *Canada* in New York harbor. This evening, Mother makes a delightful dinner of corned beef and cabbage since it is Austin's favorite. In Grandma's iron pot, we see a heavenly mixture of potatoes, carrots, and onions simmering with corned beef, making the most delightful aroma. What a wonderful sendoff we are having! Daddy gets home early so we can eat our dinner altogether as a family. Even Aunt Molly makes sure she is home on time today.

"Meg, you have really outdone yourself this evening. It looks like a great meal," remarks Daddy.

"Thank you, Paddy," Mother explains. "It is a special supper since we won't be eating altogether for some time," she says with a tear in her eye.

"I love the way you have your good dishes set up on the table on top of Grandma's lovely Irish lace tablecloth. Everything looks so beautiful, Mama," I explain.

Such a fine meal, and I can barely eat any of it as I am so nervous about tomorrow. Austin is picking at small morsels on his dish. He can't eat much; I know he is feeling poorly.

"Well, I bet you will be eating some grand meals on the ship and in Paris, and before you know it, you will be back home," remarks Daddy with a chuckle.

"Yes, and you will live in high style like royalty on the ship," proclaims Mary.

We all had a laugh at that. Of course, I manage to eat a piece of Aunt Molly's delightful apple pie, which never seems to disappoint.

"As usual, Aunt Molly, the pie is absolutely delicious," I say.

"Thanks, my darling," She remarks as she tries to give me another piece, which I cannot possibly eat.

After dinner, the dishes are done, and the kitchen is all in order. We all go to bed earlier than usual since we have to get up before dawn.

We are all up early. I don't think I slept at all. I am feeling so nervous, but I have to be courageous. We make sure we have everything all together. I have packed my diary, a copy of Charlotte Bronte's *Jane Eyre* I have to read for English class and a packet of my Latin vocabulary Miss O'Grady gave me to take along to study.

Mrs. Ryan, Danny, and Eddie are now waiting outside. It is very difficult for me to step out of our home, even though I wished many times to get away from this apartment. We have never been anywhere outside of Newark and New York City, let alone on a big ship sailing all the way to Europe.

Mother kisses me and gives me a hug. I hold her ever so close and kiss her goodbye; it is so hard to leave Mama. She is always there for me. I do my best not to cry. Saying goodbye to my mother is not easy. "I love you Mama," I say as my voice cracks.

"Here, my darling, is Grandma's St. Christopher medal. He will protect you and your brother since he is the patron of travelers," Mother explains with tears in her eyes as she kisses me tenderly.

Next, she embraces Austin and gives him a kiss and holds him ever so tightly, trying not to let him go while Daddy hugs and kisses us, too. Tears are forming in his blue eyes like pools of sparkling water.

"I know everything will be fine," remarks Mary as she too is crying and kissing us farewell.

"You, children, are like my own," says Aunt Molly as she puts an arm around each of us at the same time. "Farewell. And, Francie, if I had a daughter, I would want her to be just like you!"

"Goodbye, Aunt Molly. I love you," I respond. I am crying too.

"Before you know it, my children, you will be on the ship, coming home," replies Daddy.

"We better get going," Daddy says, trying to smile. "It is the first step that is the most difficult when we leave our loved ones."

Before we go, I pick up Collin and hold him ever so closely in my arms and give him a kiss. "Little guy, I am really going to miss you."

As we slowly go out the side door, I look back at the brownstone apartment. I guess I never realized how beautiful the old building is. I want to remember the structure and the sound the door makes when it slams. I want to remember the sound the rain makes when it hits the roof. I want to remember how the sun lights up the kitchen in the morning. I'm going to miss my home so very much and my wonderful family, whom I didn't always appreciate.

I start crying again as I see Mother through the window, sobbing into her lavender hankie. Daddy carries our suitcase outside and guides us to the trolley and then to the hotel near the dock where we are staying the night.

When we arrive at the hotel, I give my father a hug, and he says "My children, may the road rise to meet you. May the wind be always at your back. May the sun shine warm upon your face. May the rain fall soft upon your shoulders. And until we meet again, may God hold you in the palm of his hand," he adds comforting us.

After Daddy's Irish farewell, Austin and I walk into our room as I give Daddy one last kiss and hug and a final goodbye. I have never slept anywhere except my own home and in my own bed. Austin and I share a room, and we will try to sleep tonight. As I help him into his bed, I can see he is very nervous.

"Austin, can you believe tomorrow at this time we will be on a big ship traveling across the ocean? What an adventure we will have! Grandma and Grandpa came all the way to this country across the ocean to live in America on a ship like the one we will be going on tomorrow. We have their adventurous spirit, Austin, and before you know it, we will be coming home."

Soon, Austin is sound asleep. I give him a kiss and get into my bed, holding the medal Mama gave us tightly in my hand. I hope I can sleep that well tonight. In the morning, we will get up early and board the ship in a timely fashion. I can't believe that we are actually leaving. I am now thinking what Grandma used to say about life: "It really never stays the same."

Chapter 13

It is still dark when we leave our hotel. We walk quickly toward the harbor, which is just down the street from our room. There is a blustery wind blowing as we climb up the plank onto the enormous ship *Canada*. The pungent odor of fish is everywhere, and I hear seagulls cawing right over our heads as we board. Last summer, we came to the port for a joyous celebration of the arrival of the Statue of Liberty. The *Canada* reminds me so much of the *Isere*. There are smokestacks on the big ship, billowing black smoke.

As we climb up the steps, we hear the loud horn announcing our departure. How different this day is, though, since I am more anxious than enthusiastic. As we begin to move, we are actually on our way out to sea to France!

The ship is moving leisurely through the water, and we can see the buildings in the city becoming smaller and smaller as the vessel makes its way out to sea. There standing right next to us is the captain, who looks so handsome in his blue uniform and matching blue and white cap. With a big smile, he welcomes us aboard, while the deckhands take our luggage to the hospital stateroom. We follow in a singular file to see where we will be spending our nights.

The room is very stately and large. There are several beds lined up in perfect order. They are covered with crisp white sheets and fluffy pillows. The beds are so inviting since everything looks so clean and comfortable and I am so very tired. We decide to go back down to the deck so we don't miss the morning's sunrise peeking now on the distant horizon. Austin and the other boys are now sitting comfortably on their deck chairs.

There is a young nurse wearing a stiff white hat and uniform who is now covering each of the boys with a large gray blanket. The sky has become the most radiant pink and orange as we look far into the distance. I am sure this is a sight Austin and I shall never forget.

Mrs. Ryan and I grab a deck chair as we sit close by the kids. She is holding Danny ever so closely in her arms. The sweet little boy is smiling, while the wind is making his chubby cheeks so rosy. As we get further and further out to sea, the ship is now picking up speed.

"It is really getting to be a bumpy ride, Francie!"

"I know, Mrs. Ryan. I feel like I am getting dizzy. I think I should lie down a bit."

"Miss, that is the worst thing you can do," explains the nurse while grabbing two more warm wool blankets and covering us up, too. Those blankets really help since it is so cold. "You need to get used to the movement of the ship and try to eat a little. I'm Annie, and I am here to do all I can for all of you to make your voyage enjoyable. I will also be with you in Paris and on the ship back to New York as well."

"Miss, would you like something to eat? How about you, Mrs. Ryan?"

"No, I am feeling just terrible," I respond. "I feel like I am going to be sick."

"I feel rather dizzy myself," replies Mrs. Ryan.

"Stay here, and I will bring you both some soda water you can sip slowly. That should help. Your equilibrium is off since the ship is moving quickly through the water. You should just look at the horizon ahead of you. Also, try to relax. Think of something you can concentrate on that is pleasant. Try not to think of the ship's movement. That should help. I have been on these voyages many times, and you do get used to it. I will be right back."

"Here, Mrs. Ryan," the nurse says as she hands her a cold glass of water and some saltine crackers to help settle our stomachs.

"Thank you," replied Mrs. Ryan as she drinks a few sips of her water.

"Sit straight as you drink, my dear," Annie says as she hands me my water.

Taking a couple of swallows seems to help. The cold wind off the sea is refreshing and is starting to give us some comfort. I begin to drink more and more water. The crackers seem to help, too, as I am trying to concentrate on a song. Yes, I am now hearing my mother sing "When Irish Eyes Are Smiling." It's as if she is with me this very minute. Of course, I am feeling better now since imagining her singing distracts me from the nausea.

Looking far into the distance, I see crashing waves and a gigantic blue whale ahead moving right in front of us, releasing air from his lungs, which shoots up water twenty or thirty feet in the sky. How magnificent and enormous he is! I am wondering how many years he has been taking his trip across the sea. The whale gives me inspiration as I watch his elegant movement.

Suddenly, we hear a loud caw from above which grabs our attention. A lovely tern is flying high above the water. The huge bird has large white wings, a black cap, and a spot of red near his beak. He gives a sound as he flies by gracefully, and we watch as he is guiding us north on our adventure to Europe. The wind is picking up now, and the temperature is quickly dropping. Since it is freezing, we all decide to go back into the stateroom.

"How are you feeling, Austin?"

"I need to take a nap, Francie. I feel really tired."

As he lies down slowly in his cot, closing his eyes, I cover him with the sheets and blankets and kiss him on his forehead. It will be good for him to sleep for a while and rest. Little Danny needs a nap, too. Mrs. Ryan lies down next to him and quickly falls asleep as well. Strangely, I seem to have a lot more energy. I decide that a walk may help me to feel better, so I am going to explore the ship.

As I begin my discovery, I never knew there were so many people working on such a fine steamer. There are cooks and waiters dressed in clean white uniforms and caps, scurrying about the kitchen and dining hall. The dining room is so large and elegant, with lots of tables and chairs. All the tables are covered with starched white linen, and on each is a small holly plant in the center. They are so festive, with their red berries dotting the large green jagged leaves.

The floor is shining in the morning light, which is now coming through the large portholes on the far wall. Through the windows, we can see the great waves crashing against the ship. As I continue walking, I see that there are so many sailors in their navy blue uniforms and caps, walking and standing so straight and tall with their wide bell-bottom slacks, which look ever so stylish. Everyone seems to have their specific duties, which they handle with great discipline.

As I walk by, I see the captain coming toward me.

"Good day, miss. You have come with the boys to see Dr. Pasteur in Paris?"

"Hello, yes. One of the boys, Austin, is my brother," I explain.

"I'm Captain Mallory."

"I'm Francie, Francis Bridgett Fitzgerald," I say proudly, trying to stand as tall as I can.

The captain looks so dignified with his gray hair showing beneath the bill of his cap, and his black and white beard is trimmed so neatly, making his dark eyes sparkle.

"Are you giving our ship the once-over?" he inquires with a bright smile.

"You have seen the dining hall. If we walk a little farther, you will see the captain's room. Here is Benson, our telegraph officer. He gets important messages and can communicate with others as well. There is a telegraph line under the ocean between America and England, which makes messaging so much easier nowadays. Here is the compass that gives us our direction and lets us know which way we are going."

"There are lots of machines here. I guess the running of a ship is very complicated," I remark.

With a grin, the captain starts explaining all the paraphernalia. "Here is a chronometer, which measures time precisely. Next to it is our special thermometer, which tells us how cold the ocean is. Since we have two streams of ocean currents near us, we have to be very careful. There is the Gulf Stream, which comes up from the warm waters near the Straits of Florida. This goes north through the Atlantic to northern Europe, bringing warm air with it. There is also the Labrador Current, which brings cold winds down from Canada. We have to watch for icebergs, which can become very enormous this time of the year and can make it very dangerous for ships to travel, especially at night since they are so hard to see. The warm winds from the south can crack the glaciers, and huge pieces of ice can break apart, which we call calving. There is such a difference in temperature between the two currents in the ocean, which affects the types of glaciers we can get. Much of these huge chunks that come off cannot be seen because most of them are hiding under the water's surface. This section of the Atlantic we are traveling in now is called Iceberg Alley."

"The icebergs can make it very scary traveling in the ocean," I reply.

"I love the sea, Francie. I am enthralled with its vastness, power, and beauty, for sure, but there is always the fear of glaciers."

"Thank you for the tour, Captain. I best be getting back."

"I wish you and your brother the best," he politely adds.

There is more to traveling the seas than I realize. As I walk by the dining hall, I see they are starting to set up to serve dinner. I remember what Daddy said about the good food served aboard ships, as there is the most amazing pleasant smell permeating the hallway. I am starting to get a little hungry, so I decided to check on the boys and Mrs. Ryan and head back to our stateroom.

Austin is waking from his nap. Mrs. Ryan is sitting with the kids as the wait staff is bringing in their meals. The waiters are pushing carts filled with amazing aromas. They first begin with some chicken broth filled with large noodles. They are pouring the hot soup from large silver urns. It looks divine; soup is such a comfort food. The nurses are helping the boys with their dinners, so I decide to help Austin myself. Danny giggles as his mother feeds him to his delight.

Next, the waiters bring in a cart filled with white porcelain plates, which are covered with metal lids to keep the dinners warm. Each plate is filled with broiled chicken cut in half and so perfectly browned. There are also some asparagus and potatoes baked to a crisp. It all looks so delightful!

"Here, miss, is your soup," says a server as he hands me a large bowl filled with big pieces of chicken swimming in a bath of steaming broth. It is absolutely delicious and has been seasoned to perfection. My grandma would be proud! After devouring the hot soup, which is certainly what I need right now to warm me, I give Austin the chicken and vegetables, which he eats slowly.

"Francie, this dinner is so delicious!" As Austin finishes the last of his supper, he looks right into my eyes and says, "Thanks so much for being here with me, big sister. I would be so scared now if you weren't here with me."

"I love being here with you, little brother! What an adventure we are having!" I reply, ever thankful I'm making this trip with him.

Before long, it is time for the boys to get to sleep. Since the nurses are getting them ready for bed, I decide to go out on the deck. As I walk out into the cold night, there is such a familiarity to this scene I am now witnessing. There in the dark sky, I see the huge cheese-colored moon I remember from my dream from the other night in my bedroom. The stars are now shimmering in the black sky, just as I recall. The waves are crashing against the ship as the wind has intensified, and now I am freezing just like I was the other night at home.

Even though I am so scared, I cannot move away from this spot. I am so cold as there are now huge snowflakes hitting my face, but this scene seems to hypnotize me as I stand here. It is so erie! Finally, I draw some inner strength from within and make myself run all the way back to the stateroom so I can be safe and warm. I don't know what is going on with me. Slowly, I climb into my bed, crying softly, trying to warm up, hoping that the light of morning will be here soon.

Chapter 14

G asping for breath, I sit up quickly, awaking from a most horrific nightmare. I am shaking, and as I awake in the darkness, I don't know where I am. The morning now does not seem much better than last evening when I went to bed.

My dream from last night was so real and terrifying. I saw people clinging frantically to overturned lifeboats in the frigid sea and to what seemed to be parts of a ship strewn about the water. I could hear the victims crying and moaning helplessly and moving frantically in the freezing waters. And right there near them was a huge glacier that had done a most terrible deed.

In the distance, I could see a lonely life preserver, white with orange markings, but I couldn't quite make out the name of the ship that was printed on it. There in the heavens were the sparkling stars shining in the clear, cold evening, and there was that big moon again shining down on those poor souls, allowing a clear view of their agony. Thankfully, the vision was just a dream, but it was unbelievably real.

There are tears streaming down my face as I force myself up out of bed. Getting dressed quickly, I walk out of the stateroom quietly so I don't wake anyone, and I decide to go out on the deck for some fresh air to clear my mind. I look up to the sky. The stars are shining brilliantly, and there is that same moon that always seems to be near. As I stare at the heavens, I now see the lookout high on the crow's nest of our ship.

The sailor suddenly screams at the top of his lungs, "Glacier ahead!"

Suddenly, the ship is turned to the starboard side, to its right, just missing a frigid blue-hazed glacier only a short distance from where I am standing. Did I dream this? The glacier is as magnificent as it is terrifying. This huge mass of ice is a radiant indigo. What a close call! My nightmare almost became a reality. I have been completely turned around, and suddenly, I lose my balance, falling down hard on one knee on the deck.

One of the deckhands helps me up off the floor. "Are you all right, miss?" he asks.

"Yes, I am fine. Thanks," I answer as I slowly rise to my feet, looking at the massive piece of ice.

Of course, I remember my discussion with the captain from the other day. He said these waters are very dangerous when there are glaciers about or there are chunks of ice, which have been moving in the frigid sea. It could have really been bad for us today in these icy waters if the ship had rammed that glacier. Standing here now, recalling my dreadful dream, I have a most peculiar premonition, a feeling of something awful as chills go down my back.

Someday, passengers on a big ship such as the one we are on, in iceberg alley, in these chilly waters, will not be as lucky as we have been today.

Looking at the ice-cold sea with those gigantic powerful waves . . .

I begin to shiver as I remember those poor individuals that were crying in my nightmare. We are so fortunate on this vessel more than any of us will ever know. Taking a deep breath, I limp, grabbing my sore knee as I walk to the dining hall for a place to rest my leg.

A waiter brings me a cup of coffee. I'm still a little shaky. I sit at a table that faces a window so I may see the sunrise soon. I can see next to me at the table a gentleman with jet-black hair, gray sideburns, and a matching full beard. He is intently studying his sheet music and writing notes. Finally, he notices me. I don't mean to stare, but this is so interesting, and I have never seen a musician up close. Talking to him may help me take my mind off what has happened this morning.

"Hello, miss," he says with a kind smile.

"Hello," I answer softly.

"My name is John. It is so very nice to meet you."

"I am Francie. Likewise, I am sure."

"I am working on a song that I am writing for our band, and I am trying to get it finished so we can play it here on the ship before we get to France and kind of test it out on the passengers, you might say. I almost spilled my coffee all over my sheet music with that near-miss with the glacier."

"Yeah, that was a close one, for sure. I would really love to hear your music, John."

"I guess I can play what I have so far." He picks up the saxophone that was sitting on a chair next to him and begins playing the most sensational song.

My foot is tapping loudly on the floor, and the beautiful melody is making me want to march around the room. What a lively, happy sound! I feel so much better. Music can improve a person's mood.

"I haven't quite finished this, Francie. It still needs some work. We will try to play it for you before we leave the ship. Having lived in Washington, DC, during the Civil War, I have become a very patriotic musician, especially since my dad played in the Marine Band. I enjoy writing songs that make us feel good about being Americans and about being patriotic."

"How wonderful your music is! I enjoyed hearing it so much, and I look forward to hearing more, John."

As I finish my coffee, I feel that I need to give John some quiet alone time to finish his melody, so I say goodbye; and with my hurt knee, I walk slowly to the adjacent room which is a library. What a beautiful place with several dark mahogany tables and bookcases! I am amazed by all the magnificent volumes lined in perfect order on the shelves. As I take small steps around the room, I see all sorts of work for children and even medical books about various illnesses. There are more books here than I have ever seen in one place in my life. It is so amazing!

As I make it to the back of the room, I notice on the table a newspaper that is just sitting all alone, waiting for someone to pick up and read. It is an old *New York Times* from November. I take a seat on the chair, and once I pick up the paper and read the headline, I wish I hadn't.

"Louise Pelletier, Admitted to Dr. Louis Pasteur's Care in Paris, Dies 37 Days after Being Bitten by a Rabid Wolf."

How can this be? I immediately put my head down in my hands and begin to cry. Big tears stream down my face. It takes all my courage to continue reading the story.

"Even though it had been so long since she had been bitten, Doctor Pasteur had to attempt to save this poor ten-year-old child. Louise was bitten in the head. When her inoculations had been completed, she had trouble breathing and endured many convulsions. Dr. Pasteur stayed all day by her side as she lay dying."

I cannot read any further. When will this nightmare ever end? I am so afraid, still! I have to believe and have faith and be brave. I'm trying to remember what Sean and I talked about before I left Newark. I need to face the future with courage. I cannot let this news article bring any negativity to what we are trying to accomplish for Austin and the boys. So with all my strength, I need to leave this room. As I get up, I slowly fold the newspaper and place it carefully back with my shaking hands and lay it where I found it. I walk out on the deck and into the cold wind.

Feeling a little better, I go back into the dining room and ask for some breakfast. I sit, forcing myself to eat and look out at the vast ocean. Has it been too long since the boys were bitten? Will the vaccine work? I have to have positive thoughts that the medicine will cure them, and I shouldn't think of anything else. After all, the boys were not bitten in the head near the brain, as what happened to poor Louise, and it hasn't been that long ago since that terrible day when they were attacked.

A few days later, Austin and the boys and Mrs. Ryan and I are sitting on the sundeck in our chairs, covered up with our blankets, ready to look at some bright sunshine. The weather has been so cloudy and blustery. I have decided to keep silent about the article concerning Louise, so I have not told a soul about her fate.

While we are sitting here, relaxing, we see John and his band with all their instruments march out on the deck in their spectacular red uniforms. The boys are so excited to see them come out in a single file.

"Oh my, gosh, Mrs. Ryan," I remark. "That is John. I met him the other morning in the dining hall. He was working on his sheet music."

"Francie, do you know who that man is? That is John Philip Sousa and his Marine Marching Band. Can you ever imagine they play for the president!"

"Wow, I can't believe I got to meet him!"

"He writes the most beautiful American marches," she adds.

"Ladies and gentlemen," John says with a big smile, "we would love for you to hear our new march. It is entitled 'Stars and Stripes Forever.'"

As the band begins to play, my eyes are on Austin. I love his reaction as much as the music! Austin is smiling ear to ear and begins to laugh while not taking his eyes off the performance. Of course, I begin to giggle, and I have to give him a big hug as well. I am so glad he is having some fun. All the boys are cheering. Even little Danny is completely hypnotized by the music.

"Traveling is such a great experience, Mrs. Ryan. You never know whom you are going to meet or what you are going to see," I explain.

"That is for sure, Francie! I am enjoying the music."

For a moment, I have forgotten the reason why we are here on this big ship. Quickly, I remind myself that we are not on vacation. Of course, we never really forget why we are traveling so many miles through the cold Atlantic Ocean. Each day, we are getting a little closer to the medicine that will save the boys. But at least today we can enjoy the music and forget for a little while the arduous task at hand.

Chapter 15

It has been almost two weeks now on our journey across the sea, and we are all getting very excited as our ship is maneuvering its way through the English Channel, which separates the countries of England and France. I can't believe that we can finally see the port straight ahead as we are now docking in Le Havre, France. This voyage is unbelievably thrilling, as I never imagined that I would ever visit Europe.

There are so many ships in the harbor from all over the world as we can see by all the flags! We are gathering our belongings and going to be on dry land soon! It seems like forever since we left home, and I am excited and apprehensive all at the same time. Our journey continues.

We step off the boat to the smell of fish and rotting garbage in the harbor, which is now making me feel nauseated. As we clear the docks and are out in the fresh air, I get a second wind as we are getting closer to the train station, and I feel much better. We see the beautiful, ornate buildings with wide glass windows shimmering in the sunlight. How exciting!

Here we will take the train to the city of Paris. Now my feet are not touching the ground as I hear a locomotive coming to our track, number 9. It will give us transport to the city, and we will walk to the École Normale, where Dr. Pasteur does all his experiments and where he teaches. It is also the school he attended. Everyone has been talking about the great Dr. Pasteur.

As we climb aboard the train, I sit next to my little brother. "Are you enjoying the ride, Austin?"

"It is really fun! This is my first train ride, Francie."

"It's my first train ride, too," I respond. "I can't believe we will be in Paris soon, Francie. We have had quite a trip."

"Are you nervous, Austin?"

"A little."

"Dr. Pasteur is the best, and he will take good care of you. Don't worry, little brother. You will be just fine. I know it."

Saying these words out loud, I pray he will be all right. Before we know it, we are in the city. Paris takes my breath away! I've never dreamed there is such a magnificent place such as this on earth. We see the most exquisite architecture here as the buildings are tall and elaborate, with decorative edifices on each structure. It is a stylish city with wide tree-lined streets. The bare trees are decorated with sparkling Christmas lights, which glow brightly beside the broad boulevards.

No wonder they call Paris the City of Lights! Many people are walking along the avenues in long, warm fur coats, while others are sitting at outdoor cafes, sipping coffee from small cups. Would I love to stop and talk with them and have a sample of their coffee right now! No one seems to be leaving or in a hurry to go.

We see all kinds of restaurants as we walk. I smell wonderful aromas coming from all of them, which are making me so awfully hungry since we have not eaten since early this morning. There is so much to see in Paris, even in the winter. It is almost like we are visiting a different time of elegance and class so different than our Newark neighborhoods. Even New York City cannot compare to this city.

"Francie, look at those gorgeous dresses hanging in the store window! Can you believe how stunning they are?" remarks Mrs. Ryan as she walks hand in hand with each of her sons.

"I know. I can't believe how lovely they are. Would I love to go shopping and try on some of their stunning outfits!"

We hear the Parisians speaking in their most beautiful French language. We have crossed a great ocean and have arrived in a very different world. Nurse Annie is pointing out some of the wonderful sights to see. She has been with us every bit of the way, and we are so glad to have her with us today. The boys appreciated all her assistance on the ship as well. As we are walking, I see a tall arch made of stone designed with all kinds of historical scenes engraved magnificently all over it.

"This beautiful arch is the Arc de Triomphe, built under the leadership of Napoleon in honor of all the dead soldiers from all the wars the French have fought."

"How spectacular the structure is, and I can't believe people are actually able to walk through it," I remark.

We make our way for a while longer until we see a most heavenly church in the distance.

"Here next to us, you can see the Seine River, which divides Paris into two parts—the Right Bank and the Left Bank. There on the right, you can see the most stunning church, Notre Dame de Paris, also known as Our Lady of Paris."

"What a grand church," Mrs. Ryan comments.

"Look at the beautiful rose glass window with a tall spire behind it," remarks Annie. "I've been to Paris a few times, and each time I fall more in love with this city, which is by far my most favorite of any I have visited."

"What a most gorgeous church!" I say.

Annie further explains, "Here is the Café de Notre Dame, located across the street."

I added, "The café has so many people sitting outdoors. The tables are all full."

"It is considered impolite to ask anyone to leave so you can sit at a table as long as you want and sip your coffee and watch all the people going by," remarks Annie.

"Oh, that explains why no one seems to be going anywhere. What a quaint custom," I add.

"Annie, I have seen three books stores as we have been walking," I remark.

"The French people love their literature and their language. They think their language is the most beautiful in the world. To them, their authors are great heroes. Victor Hugo was one of the most favorite writers. He just died this past May. More than two million people joined in his funeral procession here in Paris, where his body lay in state under the Arc we just saw. You may have read some of his books, such as *Les Misérables* and *The Hunchback Of Notre Dame*. He had such an ability to describe his characters in such a way as though you had met them all personally and know what each and every one of them looks like."

"I have not read any of his books, but I would love to someday. There is so much in life that I have not done yet, Annie."

"Francie, you are so young. Be patient with yourself, my dear. You will accomplish everything you dream in due time."

"Annie, what is that wonderful aroma I am taking in?"

"That man over there on the corner is roasting chestnuts over hot coals," Annie replies. "It is a Christmas tradition in many European countries."

"I can see why since it smells so scrumptious."

Finally, we arrive at the École Normale. The building is as great as the others we have seen. The circular courtyard in the center of the structure is absolutely stunning. The spectacular trees are adorned with hundreds of little, white lights. How magical! I hold Austin's hand firmly, and with a smile, I escort him into the school. He has no idea how concerned I am right now for his physical well-being. My anxiety has returned, and so has the nausea.

As we walk in, I suddenly come to a complete stop. I cannot move a step farther, and here, I have to take a slow, deep breath, because standing directly in front of us is the great Dr. Pasteur. His dark hair and beard have strains of gray, making him look so distinguished and handsome. His face is so kind, putting us immediately at ease; his dark eyes are so serious while his smile is calming and caring.

He begins to speak in a direct and clear manner. "Welcome, all. We are so glad you are here today. Please come into the lab. I would like you all to meet Dr. Grancher, who will be giving the boys their inoculations to rid them of the disease. This will begin a series of daily shots until all the medicine they need has been given to them. We will work up to the strongest serum at the end of the series. We are going to begin today and start with the oldest of the boys—Willie Lane. Please, lie down and lift up your shirt and don't move."

Willie takes a deep breath and tries to lie still, staring straight ahead with his wide-open eyes looking intently at the ceiling. He seems to be really nervous. We are all a little scared. The doctor takes a needle and pricks his abdomen under the skin and leaves it there until the vaccine has disappeared out of the syringe.

Suddenly, Willie surprises us all by laughing out loud. "Why, it's like the bite of a big mosquito. It doesn't hurt a bit!" (Hansen, 2009)

I am so relieved. Next is Paddy Reynold's turn to get up on the table.

After the doctor gives him his shot, he calmly blurts out, "Is that all we have come so far for?" (Vallery-Radot, 1958)

I nervously get up to help Austin. My hands are shaking while I help him to lie down on the other bed. He lifts up his shirt to receive his inoculation. When it is over, he gives a big sigh of relief. When he is all done, I hold him in my arms, and with a soft kiss on his cheek, I help him off the table. This is the reason why we are all here and why we have made the long journey.

Afterward, Mrs. Ryan assists little Eddie up and holds his hand while he lies so still. What a trooper that little boy is. He stays perfectly still and does not make a whimper.

"Boys, you have done a great job today," says Dr. Grancher. "You older youngsters will get eleven injections in the next eleven days, with only a little each day. Mrs. Ryan, Eddie will get a total of ten because he is so young. Since there is a waiting period of a half-hour after the shots to make sure you are not having a reaction to the vaccine, you boys can have a seat in the other room and wait, please. When the time is completed, they will be taking you all to the dining hall for some dinner. I am sure you are all famished."

A cable has been sent to Dr. O'Gormon that we have arrived safely and the injections have begun. I am so glad our families will know how we are doing. The boys seem fine and are now running around the waiting room as we get ready to go to the dining hall for supper. They don't seem to be homesick at all. They have made arrangements for all of us to sleep in the hotel next door.

The days and the series of shots have gone by rather quickly. We are standing in the École Normale for the last and final day, concluding all the vaccines the boys need for their cure. Dr. Pasteur is also here, of course. He is standing next to us in his laboratory with a gleam in his eye, a big smile, and a look of relief upon his face.

"The vaccinations have been extremely successful in ridding the boys of the rabies," exclaims Dr. Pasteur. "Newark boys, please write and let me know how you are doing when you get back home to your lives. I have enjoyed knowing you all. I wish you and your families the best of luck."

I feel a great need now to speak to Dr. Pasteur before we leave. With a heartfelt smile, I put out my hand to shake his. His grip is so strong! I know I will never get the opportunity again, and I cannot let this moment go by without saying something to him.

I work up all my courage and say, "Thank you so much, sir, for you all your help, Dr. Pasteur. You are truly a great man, and it has been such a pleasure to meet you, sir."

"You are very welcome, my dear. Good luck, and God bless you and your brother and the rest of the group. Please, let us know how you are doing. Have a safe voyage home to America."

The boys have to wait in the room one last time. I am trying to remember everything so I will never forget this wonderful experience. I feel such joy today that the boys will be going home as good as new. Without Dr. Pasteur, things could have been very different. What a miracle! While we are sitting here in the waiting room one last time, about twenty Russians hobble into the building. I can't believe what I see. Some can barely walk. Each had been bitten by a rabid wolf while hunting in Siberia.

They are wearing long fur coats and tall fur hats, and all are speaking in Russian. The only word I understand is Pasteur. Some of the men are weeping out loud, and all seem to be in a great deal of pain. Each is escorted into the lab for their injections.

"Since they are peasants, Dr. Pasteur has paid for their trip here and is taking care of all their costs," whispers Annie.

"What a wonderful man he is!" Mrs. Ryan exclaims.

All the shots have been completed, and it is time for us to leave the École Normale. We need to get back to the ship as quickly as possible to sail home this afternoon, so we need to catch our train and get to the port in Le Havre. We have our entire luggage packed and are on our way. I am enjoying the scenery one last time. As we are walking, I see Mrs. Ryan bend over and grab her stomach.

"Ahh!" she lets out a loud scream and grabs her abdomen.

"Are you feeling all right, Mrs. Ryan?" asks Annie.

"I'm fine," she responds. "I just need to get home." She is walking more slowly now.

As we sit down at the train station, I take a look at Mrs. Ryan. I guess I didn't realize how big her stomach has become since we have been on our excursion. Finally the train is here. Mrs. Ryan looks relieved as we all finally board. She is walking deliberately and climbs up the steps very carefully. The train takes us to the port, where we get back on the ship, the *Canada*. We now escort Mrs. Ryan to her room.

"I need to lie down," explains Mrs. Ryan.

"I will mind little Danny for you." I pick him up and take him on the deck with me.

"Thanks, my dear," expresses Mrs. Ryan as she closes her eyes.

"Francie, that's a good idea," explains Annie as she covers up Mrs. Ryan, who is suddenly fast asleep.

I take all the boys to the deck so they can enjoy the exquisite purple sunset. Before we know it, we will be back home, and it would be nice if they enjoy their last leg of our journey.

"Francie, it is such a nice evening," Austin explains. "All in all, I have really had a good time on the trip. It is quite an experience, and before we get back, I want you to know, sister, that I am so glad you were here for me every step of the way."

"Well, Austin, it has been a great experience for me, too. It is something we will always remember together. I will forever be proud of how you handled everything you have been through with such courage. If you can handle this episode of your life the way you have, I know you can achieve anything in the future."

At this point, I, of course, have to give Austin a big hug and a kiss. "It has been a pleasure being here with you, my little brother! It has been a great time for me, also."

Looking out in the evening sky, I know all our lives have changed and will never be the same. Our prayers have been answered. In my mind, I know there is nothing I cannot do if I just put my heart and soul into the task at hand. The sea in front of me does not seem as ominous as it did before going on the trip to France. I have much more confidence that I never knew I could have as a girl from Newark. I know now there is nothing I cannot do if I just set my mind to accomplishing it. I am so looking forward to going home to my tenement.

Chapter 16

We have about a week left of our expedition, and I am so weary from being out to sea for such a long time. I want to walk on the land and see trees and sleep in my own bed. I miss my family very much and, of course, dear Sean. My diary is completely filled as I sit in the dining room by myself, thinking about everything we have done since we left Newark.

The voyage has been more than I ever dreamed it could possibly be. The thrill of meeting Dr. Pasteur and seeing the actual procedure that eliminated the boys' rabies was an unbelievable experience that I will never forget. Caring for my dear brother made me feel that I was doing something very wonderful and satisfying, better than anything I have ever done in my life.

The *Canada* has become our lifeboat, keeping us safe and taking us on a most unusual adventure across the Atlantic Ocean twice. It is both a great hotel and restaurant. The Newark traveling party has become like family, doing what is right and caring for each other in a most loving manner. As I am writing my deepest thoughts, Annie startles me as she runs into the dining hall.

"Francie!" exclaims Annie. "Do you remember when those Russians were getting help from Dr. Pasteur when we were there in the École Normale?"

"Yeah, I remember! There were many Russian peasants there. Some of them were really suffering from their awful assault by a rabid wolf."

"Dr. Pasteur saved all but three, even though it had been many days since they were attacked."

"That is so wonderful!"

"For his great efforts, the czar of Russia, Alexander II, has sent Dr. Pasteur the Diamond Cross of St. Anne for distinguished service," explains Annie. "The czar also contributed 100,000 francs to begin building the Pasteur Institute in Paris to help the world receive the great man's cures and discoveries."

"That is spectacular news, Annie," I remark. "What miracles this man has created! We were there to see some of them, and now even more people will be helped by Dr. Pasteur."

We hurry out on the deck to tell Mrs. Ryan the good news about Dr. Pasteur. She is with the boys and rocking little Danny as we hear the most lovely melody.

> Oh, Danny Boy, the pipes, the pipes are calling
> From glen to glen and down the mountainside
> The summer's gone and all the roses are dying
> 'Tis you must go and I must bide.
> But come ye back when summer's in the meadow
> Or when the valley's hushed and white with snow
> 'Tis I will be here in sunshine or in shadow
> Oh Danny boy, oh Danny boy, I love you so.

Just then, before Mrs. Ryan could finish her Irish ditty, we can see a puddle of water gushing under her chair and all around her on the deck.

"Mrs. Ryan, let's get you back to a room," remarks Annie.

"What's wrong, Mama?" asks Eddie.

Annie quickly responds, "Her water broke, and she is now in labor and about to have her baby."

Oh my gosh, the baby is coming! I am so glad Annie is here to be with Mrs. Ryan. Annie gives Danny to me and then takes Mrs. Ryan's arm, and escorts her to a private room near the hospital stateroom.

I keep an eye on the boys while we are on the deck. Dinner is being served out here now since the weather is milder than it was when we were going to Europe. I am giving Danny his supper while he sits on my lap. We're having baked cod, which comes from the Atlantic; it is absolutely delectable.

After dinner, since the temperature is dropping quickly and the wind is picking up, we all decide to go inside to our stateroom. While we are walking into the hospital room, we hear the hearty cries of a newborn baby.

Eddie screams, "Mama has had the baby!"

"Yes, she has, honey, but we are going to wait until Nurse Annie comes and gets us to see the baby. It won't be long now, boy," I respond.

After a while, Annie walks into our room with a big smile from ear to ear. "Eddie, your mother had the baby. Let's go see her. All of us can go see her since we have become such a family together."

As Annie takes Eddie by the hand, the rest of us follow the sound of a crying as I am carrying Danny.

"Eddie and Danny, you have a new baby brother!" exclaimed Mrs. Ryan. "We have named him Walter Pasteur Ryan. Come and look, my sons, and see how beautiful your baby brother is."

Eddie runs up to the bed and lays his head on his mother's shoulder.

"Mrs. Ryan, you have a beautiful little baby!" I declare.

I cannot believe how small little Walter is. I bring Danny close by so he can give his mother a hug and see his new little brother.

"Mama, can I hold him?" asks Eddie.

"Later, my sweetheart. He is awfully little right now. I know you are going to be a wonderful big brother to the little guy. Annie, can you please have the captain cable Dr. O'Gormon so he can tell my husband that he has another handsome son?"

"Of course, Mrs. Ryan," responds Annie. "It will be my pleasure!"

"Thanks for all your help, Annie," says Mrs. Ryan.

"You're very welcome, my dear. You have a handsome baby to add to your lovely family," remarks Annie. "I will also send the message that you are doing well and what courage you have, which your husband probably already knows by now."

Time is going by as we see the color of the ocean changing from a majestic blue to a lighter aqua, letting us know that the water is not as deep as it was out in the Atlantic and that we are moving closer to the shore. As we approach the harbor, I can see our lovely Lady Liberty in the distance, welcoming us back with her arm raised and her torch leading us home. What a joy to see her again! It won't be long now before we are in Newark, New Jersey, and with our loved ones.

How I miss Sean. I will be so glad to see my Mother and Father and sister Mary and little Collin, who probably has changed so much since I saw him last. I also think fondly of my dear Aunt Molly, trying to remember the fun times we've had together. More importantly, we are so thankful that the boys have been cured of their frightful, dreadful disease. We have witnessed a miracle getting the boys on the ship to Paris, cured, and back safely again. Everything we set out to do has been accomplished on our voyage. We even have a new member to our traveling party!

"Annie, since we will be back home soon, I need to speak to you for a minute privately as we step out into the hallway. I want to thank you kindly for all your help on our trip and in the city of Paris, which you made so interesting and exciting. I don't know what I would have done without your support, especially with the delivery of little Walter. You were also so incredible taking care of the Newark boys."

"It has been my delight, my dear," replies Annie. "I enjoyed the crossing very much and also being with your wonderful entourage. All of you made the trip very pleasurable for me, and the time has gone by way too fast. I am so glad I was with you all since we became the best of friends. Francie, you are a very capable young woman, and I know you will accomplish all those things you aspire. Don't ever stop dreaming and believing in yourself. As you well know, it is a beautiful, big world out there. There is nothing you can't achieve if you put your whole soul and passion into your life's purpose. You will realize everything your heart desires. It has been a pleasure to know you, and I wish you the best. I hope we keep in touch, Francie."

"Because of all you have achieved for all of us, Annie, you have inspired me to want to help others in my life just the way you have been there for our group. I am not quite sure exactly what I want to do just yet, but I have learned there is so much I am capable of doing. I am going to gain as much knowledge as I can so I can figure out what that will be. At this time, though, I am thinking I would like to work in something in the health field. You have encouraged me to care for others as you have done. Thanks again, Annie!" With that, I give her a big hug.

We see the harbor right in front of us. As we are slowly going into port now, we are getting our luggage together and saying our fond farewells. As I walk down the plank, looking at the bright blue sky, I have such a renewed energy and confidence I have never before known. My back is straight, and I am walking tall with a bounce in my step. I now know I can accomplish anything I put my mind to doing. Here, world, comes Francis Bridget Fitzgerald!

Chapter 17

I see Mama's red hair blowing in the wind, and Daddy is carrying little Collin, who looks as though he has grown so much since we have been gone. He doesn't look like a baby anymore; his hair has become so long and curly. We see our family standing down on the dock in front of the ship. Mama begins to holler and wave as she sees us walking down the steps. Mary is jumping up and down on the dock, calling out our names. Austin and I are laughing as we depart from the ship and run down the steps while I'm hanging on to our luggage ever so tightly.

I stop and take a moment to look back at the steamer once more before departing, never ever wanting to forget the memory of it and our adventures it has carried us. As we approach our loving relatives, I see tears coming down Mama's face. Mary grabs me, while Mother grabs Austin so tightly in her arms. It is so wonderful to see the Fitzgeralds again. I am overwhelmed, and I begin to cry as well.

"How are you, my son?" asks Father.

"I feel great, Daddy, but I am starving!" replies Austin.

"We will go home and eat since supper is waiting for us, dear," says Mama.

"Francie, we are so glad you are finally home!" Mary exclaims.

"I'm so glad to be back, too!"

As we walk to the ferry to take us home to Newark, I am thinking about how I felt that day when we came here to get on the *Canada*. I was so afraid of the unknown and so worried about my brother surviving his ordeal. It is so wonderful that we are finally all together and Austin and the boys are healthy..

After the ferry ride, we take the trolley on another familiar ride. I can't wait to see our apartment. In a little while, we are home. What a sight to see. The old building looks smaller than I remember. I never thought I would ever miss this place. I know I'm a different person than when I walked down those steps that cold, blustery day when we left for France.

"I'm so glad to be here!" I exclaimed.

"We missed you so much, kids," Mama replies.

"A home-cooked meal at last," Austin says with a big smile.

As we sit down for our dinner, Daddy looks at Austin and then at me as he says, "I would first like to give thanks before we eat. Dear Lord, thank you for your blessings upon this family. Thank you for making Austin well again and bringing our children home safe and sound."

"It's good that tomorrow is Saturday, and you world travelers have the weekend to rest," replies Mary with a smile.

After supper is done and the kitchen cleaned up, I get ready for sleep since I am so exhausted. In my own bed at last! I look out the window and see the stars sparkling on a clear night. They are the same stars I saw on the ocean, bidding me good night while on our voyage. The world is much smaller than I've ever realized. Life is much more of an adventure than I've ever thought, too. I rest more calmly than I did those nights before we left.

The sun is up, and so am I since I went to bed so early last night. After I have had my coffee, I need to get ready since I want to go to the store to see Sean this morning. Of course, I have to spend some time on my hair. I want to look my best today for Sean, and I put on my best coat.

My goodness, I'm so happy I'm back in Newark. It's a brisk morning, so I'm walking quickly. As I get to the market, the front door is locked, but I can see through the window Sean is bent over, placing canned goods on the lower shelves. I knock on the window. He now sees me, stands up tall, and with a big smile, runs over to unlock the door. When I walk in, we embrace and hold each other closely. I am so delighted to see Sean; it is as if I was away on the ship for months since I last saw him and looked into those beautiful brown eyes.

"I am so glad you are back! I missed you so much!"

"Sean, I am so happy to be back!"

"Francie, I get out at six today. Remember our date at Arturo's Restaurant?"

"I certainly do!"

"I will pick you up at seven, Francie."

"I have been so looking forward to our dinner, Sean I will see you later," I add with a big smile.

As I let Sean finish all his tasks he needs to complete, I decide to go for a walk. I see Dr. O'Gormon's office, and then I proceed to Mrs. Ryan's house, where all our adventures began that terrible day. A chill goes up and down my body as I look at the spot where the boys were attacked. Tears come to my eyes, remembering Austin's pain. Everything is all coming back to me as if it were yesterday, but I feel no depression since we have beaten the beast. I don't think I will ever forget that day, though. Maybe I can put those awful thoughts far in the back of my mind. Now we have so much to be thankful for, and I'm thinking I should have a little more faith than I do; I need to be more positive instead of constantly worrying about things. I know we can accomplish anything and we never really know what the future may bring. I'm excited about our date tonight, and I want to go home and leave this place and all its memories.

I have to finish my assignments for this week, so I am in the parlor working on those. I have a lot of homework to get done. The reading makes me very tired, and I must have fallen asleep on Grandma's leather couch. Mary walks into the room, startling me from my nap. I have slept for two hours, and I guess I was more exhausted than I realize. A cup of coffee sounds great so I can get something done today. Walking into the kitchen, I see Mother making supper as she always does during this time of day. She looks so physically drained; I wonder if she did not sleep while we were gone. Mama keeps coughing. I remember she had that cough before we left, but it seems to be worse.

"Hi, Mama, how are you feeling?"

"I'm good, my dear. The house is happy again since you children are finally back home. I am making corned beef and cabbage—your favorite."

"Can I help you, and you can take a nap? Sometimes a nap is the best medicine," I reply.

"That sounds like a lovely idea, my dear. Thank you."

I start getting everything ready. I have Mary help me with preparing dinner. This way, we can have a conversation, just between the two of us.

"So, Mary, how has Mama been feeling?"

"She tells me she is tired all the time."

"Well, Mary, her coloring is not very good. She looks like she has lost weight since we were in Europe. That brown skirt she wears is becoming so big on her. Every time she coughs, she grabs her chest. I should take her to the doctor on Monday and have her checked out," I reply.

The dinner is done, and we have set the table. I wake up Mother so she can eat, and maybe she will feel better after some nourishment.

"The supper looks wonderful, girls," Mother exclaims. "Thank you for your help. I am a little tired today."

"Mama, I'm going to dinner with Sean tonight. He's taking me to Arturo's for a little supper. We planned this before I left for our trip."

"It sounds like a lovely time, my girl. Sean is a nice boy and a hard worker."

I sat down with my cup of coffee. For some reason, Mother does not add milk to it. I see Mama is not eating much supper, only a few morsels of carrots and potatoes and a small piece of corned beef.

"Mama, drink some water. That should be good for you. Maybe it will help with your cough."

"Yes, that is what I need to do—drink more water. That will make me feel better."

"You know Mama, I don't have to be back to school until Tuesday. I think we should go see the doctor and see what is going on with you on Monday."

"That's a good idea, Francie."

After the meal, we don't let Mother do anything but rest. Mary, Austin, and I clean up. I begin to get ready for my date with Sean as he will be here soon. I am wearing a long black dress a friend gave me to take on the voyage. I see Sean out front, and I am so excited! I grab my coat.

"Mary, I am leaving now. Please tell Mother that I left."

"Sure, Francie."

"Hi, Francie, are you ready to go for dinner?" asks Sean.

"I sure am. I'm so looking forward to it. I thought about this date a lot when I was on the ship coming home."

Sean takes my hand, and we slowly go on our way to downtown and to Arturo's Restaurant. Thankfully, it is a mild evening and a very pleasant walk. The restaurant looks busy. As we step in, we see only a few tables that are vacant. A gentleman in a tuxedo leads us over to a small table for two in the corner and hands us each a large menu. There is a lovely Tiffany lamp with green, red, and yellow designs shimmering in the light that hangs overhead. All the tables have beautiful square tablecloths. In the center of each table is a large, lit candle; its light is glimmering in the shiny reflection of the lamp. This is more beautiful than I even remember when I looked through their front window of this restaurant a long time ago.

"What do you feel like eating tonight, my dear Francie?"

"You know, Sean, the spaghetti and meatballs sound wonderful!"

"That looks great to me also. Salad is included in the price, too."

The waiter looks dashing in his black jacket and bow tie. He takes our order and begins singing some Italian opera. I don't know what song it is, but Sean and I are astonished at the beauty of the sound and his glorious voice resonating throughout the restaurant.

"Francie, this place is amazing! I am so glad we are here."

"I find this music is so romantic, Sean," I say as I look into his eyes.

"I am so glad you are back. I missed you so much."

The waiter brings the warm Italian bread in a basket. I can't help but grab a piece and begin sampling as our salads are now on the table. The vegetables are so fresh and delicious. The dressing is incredible. Our salads go wonderfully with the Italian bread. The spaghetti plates are placed in front of us, and they look as wonderful as their aroma. Each plate has two large meatballs. Sean grabs a large spoon and begins twirling the noodles with the help of his fork. So of course, I follow his lead. It's definitely not that easy.

"Francie, I read in a magazine that is how they eat pasta in Italy."

"Sean, I didn't know you were so sophisticated," I say as I laugh.

What a pleasant evening we are having, enjoying such delectable delights. We hear more beautiful arias, and it is almost like I am across the sea again, only this time we are in Italy and I am now with Sean.

"So, Francie, tell me about your trip."

"At first, I was seasick, but I got used to the ship's movement. A very kind nurse named Annie helped me, and she was with us there and back home again. Her job was to take care of the Newark group. They had a special room for them on board. Annie was also our guide to the train to Paris and to Dr. Pasteur at the École Normale. I got to meet the wonderful man, which was such a thrill. His serum saved the boys with a series of shots for about eleven days. Sean, it was like what we said before Austin and I left, that we have to meet those responsibilities when we need to meet them. I thought of you a great deal on the trip. I appreciate your encouragement so much."

After completing our dinners, the waiter brings us some chocolate gelato, which is Italian ice cream, for dessert.

"Oh my gosh, Sean, this is the best ice cream I've ever had!"

"Isn't it fabulous, Francie? It is my favorite!"

"It is creamy and delicious and yet not heavy," I add. "The evening has been sensational, Sean, and well worth the wait."

"I loved it, too. We deserve a night out on the town considering everything you've been through and all the extra hours I have been working."

Sean gets the check and pays the bill, and then we are on our way. It is later than I think, and I need to be getting home since it's past my usual curfew and I don't want Mother to worry since she is not feeling well.

We don't say much as we slowly stroll home. We notice the wind picking up, and it is beginning to snow heavily. As we get to the apartment, we embrace.

"Thank you for the lovely evening, Sean," I say as I kiss him good night. "This evening is something I will always remember."

"Thank you, my dear, for the great time."

I walk up the steps quietly as not to wake anyone, and I shut the door, trying not to make any noise. As I hang up my wet coat on a hook in the back of the kitchen, I remember that Mama is not feeling her usual self.

I will get up early tomorrow to help.

As I get ready for bed, I have a feeling that once again I will have to be strong and diligent and meet those new challenges in my life, whatever they may be.

Chapter 18

It's Monday morning; the children have gone to school, and Daddy left very early for work. I'm helping Mother get ready to see the doctor. She has a little breakfast of tea and toast this morning. It snowed during the night, and it is absolutely freezing outside. Making sure she is ready for such a day, I bundle up mama with a hat and scarf and find her the heaviest coat. Holding her in my arms, I give her a kiss before we leave. I feel so bad that she is so sick. When I touch her forehead, it is extremely warm, yet she keeps shivering.

"Mama, Sean said there is a new health clinic just a couple of blocks down the street. We should go there since there is a new young doctor who runs it."

"Yes, I agree, honey. It's nice and close, and I don't have to walk too far."

I grab Mother's hand, and in the cold, she begins to cough even more as the fierce wind blows in our faces. Thankfully, it is only two short blocks before I see the clinic. As I open the door for her, I can't believe who I see; there right in front of us, standing in the office, is my good friend Annie in her white nurse's outfit and hat. I am so glad to see her!

"Mother, this is Annie McFarlin. She is the nurse I was telling you about who was with us on our trip. Annie, this is my mother."

"It is so nice to meet you, Mrs. Fitzgerald. I very so enjoyed being with Francie and Austin and the rest of the Newark party on the ship and in Paris."

"It is a pleasure to meet you, Annie. Francie has told me so many nice things about you and what you did for Austin. I appreciate everything you did so very much."

"Are you working here now, Annie?" I ask.

"Yes, I wanted a change and not to be traveling all the time. Here, I am close to family."

She takes us into a room and asks Mama how she is feeling. Mother describes her symptoms to Annie, who looks very concerned.

"The doctor will be with you shortly," she explains.

After her exam, the doctor tells us that Mama's weight loss, fatigue, fever, night sweats, and that awful cough she has are symptoms of tuberculosis, or as we also know it, consumption. I grab Mother and hug her so tightly; I knew she had something very serious. Tears are rushing from my eyes. Mama takes a deep sigh. I know she is worried about all of us.

"You need to be isolated from everyone, Mrs. Fitzgerald, for a while," directs the doctor. Next, he looks at me. "Young lady, everything in the home needs to be spotlessly clean including the kitchen especially, and the bedsheets and blankets as well."

"Doctor, how did my mother contract this disease?"

"TB is an urban sickness that can pass from one person to the next by a sneeze or cough. It is highly contagious. Has any other members in your family had similar symptoms?"

"No, Doctor," I answer.

"For your good and the good of all of them, Mrs. Fitzgerald, you need to be away from everybody," directs the doctor once again.

As we walk out of the exam room, we sit in the empty waiting room in front. Mother begins to sob into her hankie; I hold her once again in my arms.

"Mama, please don't cry. I know you will get better soon. You know I love you so very much. You are the best mother and someday I want to be a mother just like you."

"Francie, where am I to go? What am I to do, and what about little Collin?"

Nurse Annie walks over to us and sits next to Mother and takes her hand in hers. She has a pleasant smile and a look of confidence.

"Mrs. Fitzgerald, I have an uncle, Doctor Edward Livingston Trudeau, who is an expert on consumption. He soon will open a sanitarium at Saranac Lake to treat patients with the disease.

He provides a cottage in the Adirondack Mountains in New York for a minimal fee. His patients get fresh mountain air, rest, daily exercise, and a healthy diet. He nursed his brother with the disease, and he himself has had it, so he is well aware of what you will need to do to get better. I will write to him about your situation, and I am sure he will help you. He is a wonderful man and a dedicated physician."

"Francie, why don't you go home and get some of your mother's things together, and she can stay with me for a few days until we get her into the sanitarium. I live alone, and I have an extra bedroom. My place is just around the corner. I am going to take her there right now. It will be my pleasure to take care of you, Mrs. Fitzgerald, because Austin and Francie are like family to me."

"That is so kind of you, Annie. Can I tell my family goodbye first?"

"I don't think it is a good idea, my dear," she explains. "We don't want them getting sick, and you need complete rest. The sooner you leave, the sooner you will get better."

"Thank you so much, Annie. You are once again there for us! Mama, don't worry about anything. I will take care of everything. You need to get well. That is what is the most important." I hug Mother goodbye.

We are both crying as I leave the clinic. I have to tell everyone about Mother's condition. Aunt Molly missed work today to take care of little Collin. As I walk into the apartment, I realize that I have to be strong once more and have faith mother will get well. Collin is still sleeping, and the house is very quiet. Aunt Molly is cleaning up the kitchen as I walk into the room.

"Aunt Molly, can I speak to you?"

"Certainly. Where's Meg?"

"Mama has consumption, and she needs to be away from the kids. She is staying with Nurse Annie for a few days until she can go to a sanitarium, where she will get needed treatment. There is a doctor there who has had the disease and knows how to treat it, and she will get better, I know. The isolation is good for her, too. She definitely needs to rest, and she doesn't get much rest around here."

"I will let the O'Briens know that I cannot work for them anymore until my sister gets well. It is my responsibility to take care of everyone since you are my beloved family. You kids are the children I never had, and I love you all so much."

"Thank you so very much. I will help, too, I promise. We will get through this—that's for sure. Aunt Molly, you are the best!"

I get mother's things and put them in the old valise we used on our trip and take them to the clinic. Annie has been a godsend. What would we do without her? She is an angel once again in our lives. I'm thinking I have to tell the kids when they come home from school about our mother and, of course, Daddy late tonight.

When I return home, Aunt Molly and I start cleaning and disinfecting everything in the whole house. The linen on my parents' bed is removed and washed, and the mattresses are scoured as well. The icebox is cleaned inside and out, and so is the stove. The baby's high chair is wiped down, also. I mop the floors. Hopefully, we have removed the germs, and the disease will not spread. I must think of what I am going to say to Austin and Mary since they will be here soon. I seem to be having to do a lot of difficult things. I know I can do this. I hear the children coming in from the side door, racing as usual.

"Could you kids please sit down at the kitchen table? I have something to tell you."

"What's wrong, Francie?" asks Mary with a concerned look on her face.

"Aunt Molly and I don't know how to tell you, but Mama is really sick."

"What's wrong with her, Francie?" questions Austin.

My eyes are tearing up; I take a deep breath and explain, "We went to the clinic this morning, and the doctor said Mama has consumption, which is a disease of the lungs. She is going to go to a hospital in the Adirondack Mountains in New York for rest and exercise so she will get well."

"How long will Mama be gone?" asks Mary as she begins to cry.

"They don't know for sure, but this doctor had consumption, and he knows how to cure the disease," I explain as Austin is sobbing.

"You know, little brother, that another wonderful doctor saved your life in Paris. We need to have confidence and believe that she will get well."

"Children, I know I am not your mother, but I love you very much. I will stay here and help you with everything you need because you are like my own children. I know your mother is very strong and with all our prayers, she will come home just like you came home, Austin, good as new."

The children went to bed early right after supper since they were so upset about our Mother. Now I need to prepare myself to tell Daddy. That certainly won't be easy.

I fell asleep on the couch in the parlor, waiting for him to come home and am awakened by the slamming of the side door.

"Hi, Daddy, will you sit down with me?"

"Father, Mama is very ill. We went to the new clinic, and they say she has consumption."

"Oh no! I can't believe it. I know she has been so sick!"

Daddy begins to sob while removing his white handkerchief from his back pocket. I have never seen my father cry like that before, and so I break down too and cannot stop sobbing. I do my best to calm down, and finally, I get my composure.

"Nurse Annie has an uncle who had that disease, and he is also a doctor who has a sanitarium in the mountains in New York for people just like Mama. They get rest, exercise, and plenty of mountain air. The doctor even controls their diet. Mother is staying with Annie for a few days in town until she can get her there."

"Well, Francie, we need to get your mother well," Daddy explains as he dries his tears with his handkerchief. "God has gotten us through tough times before, my girl, and we just have to trust Him once again."

It is becoming a very long winter now, but the Fitzgeralds are taking each day as it comes, keeping busy with the hope that Mother will be home soon. We go to school, do homework, do chores, and help Aunt Molly with supper. Life does go on, and so does time.

It is Saturday morning; I must get up and get going as I drag my feet walking slowly into the kitchen, which seems too quiet and empty without our mother. I put on the coffee while tears well up in my eyes, just thinking about her. The bright red cardinal visits us very often now, perching himself on the bare oak tree out in the back. His melodic song is both beautiful and peaceful. I think it is a wonderful sign that we will all be together soon as a family. Each day is getting a little longer, too. It has been such a lingering winter, but now the crocuses peek out slowly through the slushy snow. After I sip my coffee, I remember that Sean will be here later. As I get up and get ready for the day, I hear the kids. Collin is asking for his mommy this morning.

"Mama will be here soon," replies Aunt Molly as she sits and holds him ever so closely in her arms.

Breakfast is over; Austin and Mary are outside playing in the snow. We hear a knock at the door.

"Good morning, Sean,"

"Good morning, Francie."

"Sit down and have a cup of coffee with us, Sean."

"How is everyone doing today?"

"We're fine. Did you see the flowers coming up when you came in?"

"Yes! Spring will finally be here hopefully not too much longer."

"The only problem, Sean, is we have not been informed of Mother's condition in several weeks. Frankly, I am getting concerned about her. You know they didn't want us to visit because her disease is so contagious and she needed lots of rest, so we left her alone to get well. It's been quite a while since we have heard from her even though I write to her often."

Sean can tell I'm upset. Mary opens the side door and brings in the mail.

"Francie, there is nothing from Mother," she says sadly, carrying a couple of pieces of mail into the house before going back outside again.

"Maybe someone should go down there and see how she is doing," says Aunt Molly.

"That is a good idea," I reply.

"They probably have her on such a strict daily regimen," says Sean.

"Yeah, that's true," I respond. "I know she's very busy, but I cannot help but be worried."

After a while, Austin and Mary open the side door, taking off their wet boots and coats and putting them by the radiator to let them dry.

"My dears, would you like a cup of hot chocolate to warm up with?" asks Aunt Molly.

"That would be great," replies Mary.

We are all sitting around the kitchen table. Aunt Molly is getting supper ready after pouring the kids their hot chocolate. No one says anything at all. Everyone is sitting so still and quiet.

Finally, Mary breaks the silence. "I wish Mother would come home soon."

"I know we all miss her so much. I know she's getting better, and we just have to be patient," I reply.

"But, Francie, Mama has been gone longer than you and Austin were, and you both went to Europe."

"I understand, Mary," I reply. "It hasn't been easy, but we have to keep believing."

Aunt Molly's beef soup smells wonderful. It is a good day for soup. Sean is going to stay for supper. Our aunt has made soda bread in the traditional Irish way with baking soda, raisins, and a cross on top. Everything smells so delicious. It's like Mama's here making dinner. We are so glad that Daddy is coming home early for supper and can eat with us today.

"Gosh, Molly, that soup smells so inviting!" exclaims Father as he enters the kitchen through the side door.

"Each day is getting a little longer, kids, and spring will be here before we know it," explains Daddy. "I know that is a sign that your Mother will be here soon, I am sure."

While we are eating, we hear the side door opening into the kitchen. Who could this be? Suddenly, we see Mother's smiling face. She looks so much better!

"Oh my God, Mama is home!" I scream.

There is Mother smiling with her cheerful demeanor escorted by our friend Annie, who is also beaming.

We all run up to her. Austin, Mary, and I are grabbing Mama all at once. "Let me take your coat, my dear." Daddy kisses her and holds her ever so close. "Welcome home, Meg," he adds.

Collin is squealing as Molly picks him up from the high chair and carries him to his mother. The boy leaps into Mama's arms, laughing. Mother is crying a happy cry, and so am I.

"Annie, let me take your coat. Please join us for supper," I say.

We all make room around that faded kitchen table. This simple meal has been the most wonderful dinner we have ever eaten. Tears of joy go down my face. Mother is finally home, and we are complete again.

"Daddy, I would like you to meet Nurse Annie. She was there for Austin and the boys on the ship and home again. We also need to thank her for her kindness in helping Mama in her time of need."

"It is very nice to meet you, Annie. You are always welcome in our home. Thank you for all you have done for the Fitzgeralds," replies Daddy.

Aunt Molly gets up and brings out the chicken leftovers and makes sandwiches for all of us.

"Please, everyone, help yourself," directs my aunt.

"Annie, your uncle is a great doctor," explains Mama. "He cleared my lungs, and I put some weight back on. I have so much more energy now than before when I was so sick. He was a godsend."

"Yes, he is a great physician. We are so proud of him, that's for sure."

"Annie, you have influenced me a great deal," I say slowly. "The way you handled everything on the ship and on our way to the hospital in Paris, I think you are a remarkable woman. It was so amazing the way you took care of Mother, too. Someday I wish to have your knowledge and ability to help others the way you have helped our family. I want to be a nurse just like you, Annie."

"What kind words, Francie! Thank you so much."

"You can do anything, my girl," replies Daddy. "I would be so proud of you getting an education and becoming a nurse."

"What this family has been through, I know my girl, there is a plan out there for all of us," explains Mama.

As we are finishing our supper once again all together, Sean says, smiling as he takes my hand, "I'm so happy you are going into the medical field just like me Francie!"

"Welcome back, Mrs. Fitzgerald," Seàn remarks as Mother is enjoying her dinner.

"Thank you, Sean. It's so good to be back," Mama replies.

Yes, as I look around the old kitchen table, I can see that we are all now so relieved and thankful to have Mother in our presence once again.

I hear the red cardinal calling me as he sings on the oak tree in the yard. As I am looking out the window, I suddenly see a vision of myself walking into a hospital. I am wearing a nurses outfit and as I enter the building, I see Sean smiling from ear to ear wearing a long, white doctor's coat. I know Francis Bridget Fitzgerald you are destined for something grand!

Bibliography

Hansen, B. (2009). *Picturing Medical Progress from Pasteur to Polio.* New Brunswick: Rutgers University Press.

Mann, J. (1964). *Louis Pasteur Founder of Bacteriology.* New York, NY: Charles Scribner's Sons.

Parker, S. (1993). *Science Discoveries Louis Pasteur and Germs.* London, England: Belitha Press.

Smith, L. W. (1997). *Louis Pasteur Disease Fighter.* Sprinfield, NJ: Enslow Publishers, Inc.

Vallery-Radot, P. (1958). *Louis Pasteur A Great Life In Brief.* New York: Alfred A. Knopf.

About the Author

Victoria Olivett taught 7th Grade Middle School for thirty-five years in Lansing, Michigan. She has a degree in Sociology and History from Michigan State University. She enjoys making history come to life so others have the opportunity to relive experiences from the past. Victoria believes that history empowers us to learn from one another and affect change positively. She has traveled many places in the world and has a passion for learning and speaking different languages.

Victoria received an Honor Award for service to St. Jude's Children's Research Hospital from Danny Thomas. Victoria was born in Detroit, Michigan and currently lives in Gurnee, Illinois. She enjoys spending time with her husband Daniel, three daughters, and eight grandchildren. She also loves going for long walks and reading.

Prospect Heights Public Library
12 N. Elm Street
Prospect Heights, IL 60070
www.phpl.info

CPSIA information can be obtained
at www.ICGtesting.com
Printed in the USA
LVHW112026181021
700772LV00005B/274

9 781941 049082